Sweetland
of Liberty
Bed & Breakfast

A novel

Donna Cronk

Sweetland of Liberty
Bed & Breakfast
A work of fiction
Copyright © 2014 by Donna Cronk
Cover art created by Marilyn Witt

This is a work of fiction. All people, places, events, businesses, and organizations mentioned in this book are either the creation of the author's imagination or used fictitiously.

Available on Amazon.com, Createspace.com, and by writing the author at: 8754 Carriage Lane, Pendleton, IN 46064.

ISBN-13: 9781493570362
ISBN-10: 1493570366
Library of Congress Control Number: 2013920026
CreateSpace Independent Publishing Platform
North Charleston, South Carolina

For Brian, alive and well.
With love and gratitude.

Contents

Sweetland of Liberty

Bed & Breakfast

Sometimes you have to move back to move forward.

ONE

Change

SAMANTHA JARRETT GRABBED HER boss's tote bag and scurried to catch the elevator before the door closed.

"What would I do without you, Sam?" Dr. Joanna Reeves asked as the door slid shut and they began their descent to the lobby. It was a rhetorical question, one that Joanna had been asking for a decade. And one that always resulted in a smile and slight shrug from Sam.

While serving as executive assistant to the president of small Frankfort College in upstate Ohio was fulfilling, and Samantha enjoyed it, there was much more to it than that. Ever since her husband died two years ago, the job was vital. Roger was forty-eight when the aneurysm took him suddenly. Sam was the same age, and in a way, her life—at least life as she knew it—ended that day too. This job gave her a reason to get up in the morning, and even more, the days were so demanding that at the other end of the clock, her work provided the gift of exhaustion, which meant sleep; some nights, anyway.

Sam also needed the income. It was a shock to find that Roger's death-benefit package had a loophole the couple had overlooked until Roger's passing. Who even thought about such things, especially at their age—unless they were suddenly needed? The short of it was that she wouldn't retire early, to say the least. In fact, looking ahead, she'd have to work longer than most everyone she knew. Funny how people occasionally made thoughtless comments about her becoming "a rich young widow." She wasn't young, and she certainly wasn't rich.

"Here's your bag," Sam told Joanna as the women ducked into the ladies room to freshen up before the big speech.

Joanna was pushing sixty and had delivered many annual state-of-the-college speeches in her years as the school's leader. Both Joanna and Sam knew the drill for this first Friday morning in February as they walked to the auditorium and sat alongside college-administration dignitaries.

Sam took her seat at the president's right hand, available to assist with mobile communications and whatever else was needed by the president. Meanwhile, the students and college faculty filed in; at precisely eleven, Dr. Reeves strolled to the lectern. She reviewed the college's most notable accomplishments of the last twelve months, and previewed what was ahead.

Sam looked out over the crowded auditorium thinking of how she would soon walk to the presidential mansion for a lovely catered reception. After that, she and the president would spend the afternoon back in the administration building catching up on their considerable workload.

Joanna had been out of the office for a few days on personal business and said she used a block of that time to assemble today's speech. Most years she previewed it with Sam—but not this one. It was odd, but Sam didn't dwell on the change in routine. Instead, her mind rushed to the busy afternoon ahead. It appeared that Joanna was about to wrap up her speech. Sam picked up a pen to take notes; not jottings about the talk, but rather a to-do list for the rest of the day.

"And furthermore," the president continued, "I have every confidence that this college will move forward as I prepare to leave it behind."

Leave it behind?

Sam looked up from her notes. "That is why it is with regret, yet also a keen sense of pride in the work we have accomplished here together, that I announce my retirement as your president, effective on April 1."

The crowd reacted with a collective murmur. This wasn't something attendees were expecting. There was no tip before this moment that anything out of the ordinary was coming, and certainly not that the Dr. Joanna Reeves era was ending. Sam's pen dropped to the floor. An

English professor sitting next to her picked it up. "When did she decide this?" the professor whispered.

"I—I don't know," Sam answered, dazed.

Some moments later, Sam found herself on her feet, clapping along with the rest of those in the building as the president greeted officials and made her way next to Sam. The school song played as the auditorium emptied. "Well, that is that," Joanna said, holding out her hand to Sam, a motion she often used to indicate that she wanted her cell phone. Sam obliged, trying to lock eyes with her boss. Joanna avoided the contact.

Sam summoned every ounce of poise she could muster to walk normally off the stage behind Joanna, who was being approached by several people as they all moved toward the door.

Confused, hurt, angry—the emotions collected in a heap. Sam swiped her forehead as if to flick off the headache that was forming. The new president would bring his or her own staff; everyone knew that's how it worked. The last thing he or she would want around is the former president's assistant.

By early spring, Joanna would be retired. And Sam would be unemployed.

Sam felt ill. She certainly had no appetite for the roast beef and green beans at the buffet reception. She picked at her salad and prayed that no one grilled her with questions. *It was embarrassing.* As Joanna's right-hand woman, she should have been told first about her boss's plans.

How was she supposed to answer the messages coming in on her cell? Local reporters were learning about the story via social media. Normally, she would have prepared written releases about any breaking college news. Today, she was as in the dark as they were. Sam couldn't wait to get out of there and back to the office. She had plenty of questions of her own.

Finally, they were alone in the president's quarters. Sam walked into Joanna's inner office and closed the door. Choking back tears, her questions flooded the room in a continuous stream. "Why didn't you tell me that you were retiring, Joanna? How long have you known? What are we going to tell the media? I—I just don't understand your timing in all of this."

Joanna still wouldn't meet her assistant's gaze, and instead, glanced past Sam, eyes darting around the room, landing back on the paper work at hand. "I have prepared a statement and just e-mailed it to you. Share that with the media and everyone else who asks," she said matter-of-factly.

"Samantha, I didn't know how to tell you about my decision. In all honesty, I haven't known how to approach you with anything of an emotional content since Roger died. I felt it best to simply make the announcement and get on with it. I think that about covers it now, don't you?"

With that abrupt dismissal, Joanna swirled around in her chair, turning her back on her longtime assistant. *What would Dr. Reeves do without me, indeed,* Sam thought.

"Joanna, you know what I have been through," Sam said to the back of her boss's head. "It has been difficult since I lost Roger. You know that I need this job. Why couldn't you have given me a heads up that I would be losing it?"

The president turned back around and this time answered Samantha's question directly. Her blue eyes were cold. Sam knew at once there was no empathy coming her way. "Excuse me, Sam, but I did give you that 'heads up' that you mentioned. You still have some weeks left here to work. I think that is plenty of time for you to figure out what you want to do next.

"Look, I know what you have been through, and while I am sorry for that, I am not responsible for your employment beyond my tenure, nor am I responsible for your overall happiness. Now, if you will excuse me, I have things to do."

Samantha left the office and shut the door quietly behind her as she went. She was so angry that she nearly kept walking out of the building to leave for the afternoon. But doing that would only prove Joanna's point about emotion. She would finish the day, make some notes about Monday's speech, and make sure that all interested media had the release Joanna had prepared alone.

Sam knew too well that life could turn on you. And once again, it had.

She held her tongue the rest of the afternoon, counting the minutes until she got to the safety of her Green Hills home and had the weekend to regroup.

⁓

THE WELL-KEPT TWO-STORY HOME was in a nice suburban neighborhood and took just outside half an hour, on a good day, to reach from the college campus. It had been the Jarrett family home for twenty years, purchased after Roger got a big promotion when their two sons were small. It held the boys' childhoods as much as it still housed Roger's exercise equipment, fishing tackle, and the couple's antiques, handed down from both sides of their families, and collected here and there, besides.

Sam brewed a cup of green tea as snowflakes drifted onto the driveway, and started to pile. Night fell early on Ohio winter days. She folded herself into Roger's favorite chair, a large, worn, brown-leather number that enveloped her into the soft seat as she buried herself in a handmade, crocheted afghan, a recent Christmas gift from her sister-in-law, Jenny.

The house, the tea, the chair, and the blanket were all comforting. But they weren't enough. Sam needed a sympathetic ear. *She needed Roger.* She had restrained herself from spilling it all out to a friend on the drive home. She thought it best to release this news in some sort of pecking order, starting with her older son, Ray.

At twenty-seven, he was a newlywed of several months. He had met his wife, Sally, at the St. Louis law firm soon after he came on staff. She was an interior designer and was working in his building at the time, helping with a redecorating project. It was nearly love at first sight.

Sam dreaded calling her sons with any kind of sad news. She wanted only to share good things with them. The horrendous memory of telling first Ray, then Gus, that their father died made her feel like the Grim Reaper. And here she was, with more bad news. She caught Ray while he was driving.

"Ma! I didn't expect to hear from you at this time of day. What's up?"

"Kid, I got some difficult news today. Joanna is retiring. She didn't even tell me first or anything—just announced it during a public speech. I'm still reeling."

"You've got to be joking, Mom," Ray said. "That's a heck of a tough break. All those years you've been with her. It doesn't sound like your boss; not the Joanna Reeves you've spoken of for so long. What's your next step?"

"I haven't gotten that far yet, Ray," Sam said. "I'm going to have to give it some thought, let it all sink in. I just don't know how to even look for a job these days. The campus has a hiring freeze for one thing. It's a sure bet the next president won't want me there."

Ray agreed that she was likely right. "Mom, listen, I'll talk to you later. Right now I'm pulling into the parking lot to meet Sal for dinner. Promise; we'll talk later. Love you."

Sam wished she hadn't bothered him right then. She didn't know what she expected her son to say, what measure of comfort he could even offer. But he was in a hurry and seemed distracted.

Her younger boy, Gus, recently relocated to Denver, and with the time difference was still at work in his new position directing an art gallery. It was his first real post-college job after bouncing around working in coffee shops and trying to sell his paintings. At twenty-four, he couldn't be more different from Ray if he tried.

Ray was serious and scholarly, methodical and driven. Gus was willing to take chances, ones that frightened someone like Sam, who always sought the predictable, the safe. But he was also pure sunshine, a young man of fun and possibility.

Even as a girl, she went for the guys like Ray, and like Roger; the ones who designed their paths to success and rarely veered from their long-term goals. Gus had a big show opening at the gallery this weekend, and Sam knew he would be busy with tonight's reception. It was a big deal. She wouldn't bother him. Not now. What was she even thinking, she had to wonder, impulsively calling Ray and thinking about phoning Gus. Her problems were her own, not her kids' issues to sort out.

Frustrated, and finally hungry, Sam fixed herself a peanut-butter-and-jelly sandwich and a second cup of tea. The snow was coming down hard, now, and she was glad she was home. She watched the large flakes fall, backlit by the street lights, and finished her meal.

Only then, finally, did she allow herself the luxury of a good cry.

She wondered which would stop first: the snowfall or her tears.

TWO

Freedom

IT DIDN'T MATTER THAT the snow was stacking. Weather was the least of Sam's worries as she had no plans to leave her house all weekend. The white stuff wasn't generally a problem in northern Ohio. Everyone expected and prepared for it. It wasn't like in her hometown of Freedom, Indiana. Sam wondered if getting around back home was still as difficult as it was growing up on the farm outside of town. A good snowstorm could shut down rural, hilly United County for days.

Suddenly nostalgic, she pulled up from the Internet the current issue of her hometown weekly newspaper, *The United Times*. The paper still led with county commission meetings and winner of the spelling bee. But what caught Sam's eye was a photo of two women jointly holding a plaque for donating funds to the United County Business and Cultural Forum. They were June Foster, town matriarch for all of Sam's life and then some, and Ellen Madison, who worked for June's business, Foster Foods of Freedom, and went through school with Sam.

Mrs. Foster had to be at least eighty. In fact, she was eighty-two, to be exact, after Sam did the math. She graduated from Freedom High School with Sam's late father, Herb Jones. Mrs. Foster's name came up a couple of years ago during Sam's thirtieth class reunion. They were all talking about how the town never changes, and Roger mentioned that moving there might be a good fit for retirement. The comment stunned Sam because while it was a hidden desire of her heart to at least *consider* that option, she didn't know until then that it was something Roger had thought about too.

That reunion night, Sam's school-days chum, Angie Gray, leaned across the banquet table. "You and Roger should look into buying the Foster place," she said. "Word is that Mrs. Foster isn't going to hang onto it too much longer, and she has no one in the family to take it."

It was Sam's favorite house in her hometown. Truly, it was probably everyone's favorite. The place had been the anchor property of little Freedom for two centuries. The Fosters were the county's largest employer. It was unimaginable to think of Freedom without June Foster, or at least, without *some* Foster, living in the landmark set deep into three lots on North Main Street.

"I remember how you loved that place, Sam. Every day when we left school and passed it on the bus, you had your face plastered against the window. Half the time you wouldn't even talk to me until we went by," Angie recounted.

Sam couldn't stop thinking about the paper's photo of Mrs. Foster and about the reunion night when Roger insisted that they drive by her place. That evening, he pulled over and cut the engine, and the two of them had sat and stared at the old white two-story with its deep-green window shutters and massive wraparound porch.

"You know what we should do?" Roger had asked, suddenly animated. "We should buy it. Yep, turn it into a bed-and-breakfast. So much of my work is done by computer and business trips anyway. I don't have to live in Green Hills. I can live anywhere. The boys are grown and gone. You could run the place. We'd be home together most of the time. What do you think, toots?"

This was Roger talking? The idea certainly was intriguing to Sam.

They hadn't told anyone about their musings. For one, they hadn't had the time. The idea was, for Sam, like some wonderful secret that had only begun to take hold of her heart; like expecting your first baby in those tender days before telling anyone, but knowing that the joyful news is there, ready to burst forth and share with others, and that with each telling, the words will bring new delight all over again.

Sam and Roger loved visiting country inns and always commented to each other about aspects of the places they liked, as well as how they would do things differently if they owned them. In the years since the boys had left home, they had taken to spending quite a few weekends in midwestern towns to visit antiques shops and festivals. They always sought out the small B and Bs. They discussed the menus, the furnishings, and the hospitality.

But her very own bed-and-breakfast? In the Foster house back home in Freedom? Could this be the Lord's plan? It was too outlandishly wonderful to even dream about.

Then Roger died and Sam grieved—still grieved—so hard for him that until this moment she had not even given another thought to that short-lived daydream that the two of them held silently, and so briefly before his sudden death.

And now, Sam bore another loss. Her career was finished. At least the one she had worked so hard to establish with Joanna. Apparently, Joanna had dreams of her own that she hadn't shared either.

As painful as it was to think about losing her job, and having to figure out a new way to make a living, what stabbed Sam like a knife in the back was the way she was treated by Joanna: the icy look in her eyes when Sam tried to speak with her privately; the way Joanna cut her off and literally turned her back. This was not the Joanna that Sam had known for a decade. Maybe she didn't know her boss so well after all. In fact, she wondered what she knew about anything.

Sam stared out at the cold night, and started weeping again as she watched the snowflakes continue to stack. *Oh Lord, where are you? Have you left me too?* she prayed silently. *I'm so afraid. Please show me your plan.*

It had been a hard day. As exhausted as she was, Sam found herself unable to settle her mind enough to sleep. She dug out from her late mother's cedar chest the old high-school scrapbooks, a box of decades-old photos, and the *History of Historic United County* hardback book that the historical society had printed as a fundraiser decades ago during the county's sesquicentennial.

She read about the Foster family members, and how the first of them settled in Freedom before it was even named Freedom. Hank Foster opened a trading post, and the Indians came around to exchange goods. From the start, the Fosters were seen as trusted, fair businesspeople.

Much later there came a food warehouse and distribution center, and for a whole lot longer than Sam's lifetime, Foster Foods of Freedom employed a large number of residents.

The wealthy Foster family could go anywhere but was committed to Freedom. Even today, the Fosters remained well respected by employees and clients alike.

Sam spent much of her weekend immersed in the past. When she was finally able to rest, the dreams came. She dreamt that she read in the hometown newspaper about the Foster house being for sale; that she and Roger bought it. Just like that, they started a whole new life. She woke herself up laughing softly at Roger, who in her dream was cracking some joke while painting the Foster kitchen a particular shade of yellow. But when reality hit, and she fully awakened, there was nothing funny.

By Sunday morning, Sam realized that she had not gotten out of her Friday-night pajamas and wool socks and decided *why change now?* She half expected for Joanna to call her during the weekend and apologize. Sam thought her boss might say something like: "Samantha, I don't know what got into me. I was rude to you and I'm sorry." But there was no call. Ray never phoned her back, either. She skipped church; let the machine get the landline when it rang twice. She fought off the desire to bother Gus in Denver.

She was in a pretty terrible mood and decided it best not to inflict herself on anyone she cared about. Since Roger had died, she was always so pitiful. Sometimes she saw the pity people felt for her all over their faces.

∽

THAT AFTERNOON, SAM FELL soundly asleep on the sofa, and after a two-hour nap, her eyes shot open and she knew something then that she had not known two hours earlier:

This is it.

This, right now, is my fresh start.

She'd lost the love of her life. The boys were raised, moved away, and on their own. She was without a job, or at least would be, very soon.

Nothing, really, held her here. She had great friends, but they were busy with their jobs and their families most of the time. She had to work, that much was certain. So why not go for that dream that she and Roger had nurtured together so briefly? It might be crazy, but she could at least give it a shot, couldn't she?

She wouldn't tell anyone her plans. If she did, someone, for sure, would talk her out of them. She could hear it now: "It's ridiculous," someone would say. "A woman your age moving away and taking on an old house by yourself? How do you even know that there is enough overnight traffic in Freedom to support a bed-and-breakfast? And even if there is, could you possibly afford to buy a house like that?"

Sam thought maybe it was high time that she did something a little, well, unconventional; take a chance at something bigger than herself. While fifty wasn't young, it wasn't old, either. There was time to begin again. She packed an overnight bag and decided that before Monday's light she would drive the 554 miles to Freedom. In fact, she wouldn't even notify Joanna until the morning. It had stopped snowing, and the weather report on her cell phone showed that the further southwest she would go toward Indiana, the lighter the snowfall would be.

She would do it. She would ask Mrs. Foster if she could buy her home.

If they struck a deal, then Sam would open her own inn. And she would paint the kitchen a particular shade of yellow: the very same color that Roger had chosen in the dream.

Their vision was alive again in her alone. And for the first time in—a long time—Sam was more alive than she could remember.

ᐁᔤ

THE OLD CUCKOO CLOCK sounded at 4:00 a.m. They'd had that clock for years, inherited from her in-laws, and Sam was so used to it that it never awakened her; except that it did today. She didn't wait for the alarm clock to beep at four thirty, but instead bolted out of bed with the bird. She couldn't recall a time when she felt such ridiculous clarity about anything like what she was about to do.

Sam had always lived a cautious life. She got her mammograms and her dental exams on practically the exact calendar dates they were due. She almost never missed work, even when she felt so ill she could barely hold up her head. She did what was expected of her and when it was expected.

But what had all of that gotten her? A dead husband whom she missed mightily; nights alone so frightening that she cried herself to sleep while sobbing into a pillow; family members who lived so far away that she saw them only on the occasional holiday. And now, she would be unemployed, and the boss for whom she had labored for a decade hadn't even shown her the courtesy of telling her about it in private. She'd had to hear it with everyone else.

Come to think of it, Sam couldn't recall ever skipping a day of school or work. She had never even considered it, really. But today, a busy Monday morning, she was missing work on a strange whim, and it felt exhilarating. She got herself dressed while it was still dark, stepped into her old, dependable Jeep, and started out on the long drive.

She waited until eight, her normal arrival time at the office, to call her boss. There was some satisfaction in this. She knew the call would take Joanna aback. Good old Sam, Joanna always thought. Well, not today. She didn't *ask* for the day off, either; or apologize for claiming it.

"Joanna, I won't be in today," Sam said. "I am taking a personal day."

She spoke in simple, declarative sentences.

"But Samantha, we have some things to see to right away. Is something the matter? Do you suppose you could come in around noon then?" Dr. Reeves asked, obviously flustered. "We have the fundraiser dinner tonight, and you were going to brainstorm with me some thoughts for my after-dinner remarks. You never take unscheduled personal days. I need you here, today," the president said.

"Well, Joanna, I need to be *here* today," Sam answered. "This is my life too you know. I'm sure you will manage just fine without me. Maybe you could ask Terri from downstairs to help out. She writes well and can assist with your speech. The thing is, I need tomorrow off too. I'll see you Wednesday."

She could tell that Joanna wanted to keep discussing the absence, but Sam didn't give her a chance. Sam ended the connection and kept driving, empowered in a way that she had never been before.

As she drove on, Sam laughed aloud with a thought: *What's she going to do, fire me?*

THREE

The Foster House

BY EARLY AFTERNOON, SAM approached the sign, *Welcome to United County*.

Instead of driving straight into Freedom, she impulsively hung a right on a familiar county road, then a left until the gravel led past the small, old farmhouse where she was raised. There was a newer swing set in the side yard, and Sam couldn't help smile at the notion of a young family calling the Jones homestead its own. She continued on, passing the snow-covered fields where her father had raised corn and soybeans. She passed the woodsy pond where she and her friends swam in the heat of so many summers. Memories flooded her mind like sunshine on a warm day. But it wasn't a sad kind of nostalgia. Curiously, it was a sense of hopefulness.

Finally, she wound back to the main highway and drove the few miles to the edge of town where the Foster Foods complex was located. The parking lot was full of employees' vehicles, and that, too, made Sam happy. Business appeared to be thriving. She drove into Freedom town limits, past the John Whetsel law firm, past the dentist's office, past the elegant limestone courthouse centered in the town square, and past Frame's Real Estate.

She pulled up to the prettiest house in the residential district of North Main Street and parked her car. But before she got out, she paused to ask for support. *Father, I don't know if my being here now is all you or all me, but I ask for your will to prevail. Lord, if I'm to get this house, let it be so. But if it's not what you want, please help me to get over it. Amen."*

With that, she walked up to the door as though June Foster expected her. It was a bold move; not something most people would consider doing—just showing up with no appointment, no warning, no nothing but a fire in her gut that fueled her forward. She was risking everything right now—her dream, her future, her finances—even her remaining time employed with Dr. Reeves. As Sam rang the doorbell, she didn't even pause to catch her breath. She was running on adrenaline.

No one answered right away, but Sam was unfazed. If she had to, she'd stand there all day. She was in too deep, had driven too far, to get to this point without following through. Besides, if she turned around now, she would never show up here again. This was her moment, one way or another.

As she waited, Sam looked around. The house was even larger viewed from the massive porch. Behind it, the rooms stretched deep into the backyard. It needed some work, which surprised Sam, but still, it was magnificent. Even after all these years, and all the places she had traveled and inns in which she had stayed, this had remained her favorite house of them all.

Finally, the door opened slowly, and to Sam's surprise, it was June Foster herself, an elderly woman, yes, but you could see the spark remaining in her eyes. The two women stared at each other for a long moment.

"Mrs. Foster?" Sam asked. "I know you won't remember me, but I'm—"

"For land sakes, child, of course I remember you! I would know you anywhere!" Mrs. Foster said. "You are Samantha Ruth Jones! You are the spitting image of your father!"

"Actually, my name is Jarrett now, I mean, was, am—well, you see, my husband Roger passed away two years ago."

Mrs. Foster offered her condolences and continued. "You will always be a Jones in my eyes. We can never escape our roots or our genes, and my dear, look at you. You certainly have the genes of Herb Jones!"

Samantha remembered that during her father's funeral, Mrs. Foster had paid her respects and shared with Jones family members the stories about how Herb was the first boy on whom she had a crush.

"So how are you doing now, Miss Samantha? Wait. Please excuse my manners. Won't you come inside, dear? It's far too cold to be visiting in the doorway."

Samantha stepped into the Foster home for the first time ever and released a soft sigh. The spacious foyer featured a grand staircase ahead to the right that extended to the second floor. On both sides of the stairs were parlors. Mrs. Foster motioned to the right parlor into which the two women walked, taking seats in floral wingback chairs that faced each other at an intimate but not uncomfortable distance, just right for good conversation.

"So this is the beautiful Foster home!" Sam offered. "Mrs. Foster, you have no idea how many times I have passed your house and wondered what it looked like inside. This sounds silly, but while some people dream of visiting sandy beaches or seeing some fabulous city, I have always imagined being right here."

Mrs. Foster chuckled. "Well, I do hope that you are not disappointed, Samantha. It's an old house and I am an old woman, and I'm afraid that even with good help like Joanie, I don't always see to everything that I probably should. It's a lot of house for one person."

"I'm anything but disappointed," Sam said. "Truly, I'm more intrigued than ever."

"Would you like to see the rest of it?" Mrs. Foster offered.

"That would be wonderful," Sam said.

The two women made their way through the stately old house. They passed through the dining room, the large, comfortable kitchen, the private suite in the back of the house where Mrs. Foster now both relaxed and slept so that she didn't have to navigate the stairs.

"I would take you up or have Joanie accompany you, but I'm afraid she's out to the market and I no longer take the steps, Samantha."

Mrs. Foster told Sam about the four large bedrooms upstairs and the attractive library sitting area into which each of the guest rooms opened.

It was all overwhelming for Sam. What would prompt this woman to give her a detailed tour of her private home and not even ask why she was there? And the house—it was even more ideal than Sam had imagined it could be for turning into a well-appointed small-town inn. She was beside herself with excitement. Her heart was about to pound out of her chest in anticipation of what she would propose later this day when the time seemed right. She only hoped that Mrs. Foster couldn't hear it beating so loudly.

"Samantha, would you like a cup of tea? The water is still hot."

"I would love that. Thank you, Mrs. Foster."

"I don't suppose you would care to retrieve it for us, would you? I'm a bit tuckered out from the house tour."

Sam was happy to help. She got up and walked to the kitchen where she found the tea service on the counter and the kettle still hot on the stove. She looked around and imagined herself pouring tea, baking cakes, and serving breakfasts in that very room. It felt exactly right. But to be perfect, she imagined this wallpapered room painted *yellow*.

After they chatted for a while longer and poured themselves second cups, Mrs. Foster finally asked her the question. "So what, may I inquire, brings you to my door, Samantha?"

Sam took a deep breath and got right to the point.

"Mrs. Foster, this may not make any sense to you, and I will have to say I feel like I am in a dream right now sitting in your lovely home. I have led a very predictable, cautious life, and in this life, I have lost my husband, and now I am losing my job. I feel that I really don't have anything else to lose, so I have decided to simply come here and tell you what I would like."

June Foster listened and sipped her tea.

Sam continued. "Well, what I would *really* like is to have my husband and my job and carry on as usual, but since those things are no longer possible, I will ask you for the one thing I want in this world that is possible—or might be, anyway."

With that, Sam took a second deep breath. This was it. "Mrs. Foster, I would like to purchase your home. I would then turn it into a bed-and-breakfast."

Now Sam was silent too. She decided to let the quiet hang there for a moment in all of its intensity. The sun shone through the lacy curtains in the opposite parlor, and left a patterned trail of warmth on the foyer's polished, golden-oak floors.

"Well, this is most unexpected," said Mrs. Foster, laughing softly. "You won't believe this, but actually, a sign is to go into the front garden very soon listing my home for sale. I am set to do the paper work next week with real-estate man Dan Frame in John Whetsel's law office."

Samantha felt her heart sink. But she still had to give it her best shot.

"Mrs. Foster, you do what you have to do, and sign what you have to sign. But before that time comes, I just need to tell you that I love this town. I love this house. If I lived here, I would help take care of them both. All of my adult life I have wondered what it would have been like to raise my children where I was raised and to make my life with the people who share my roots.

"Roger, my late husband, and I dreamed of returning here and opening a bed-and-breakfast. But then he died, and while I wish at times I could too, well, I really don't know what I am doing, but I'll tell you this much. I can write a check to you right now for every dime I can spare, and I will write another for every additional one that I can scrape together. That is, if you choose to sell me this house.

"It scares me to ask you this, but it scares me more to let this house get away forever without trying to buy it. This is the only dream I have left. It was *our* dream. I want to pursue it with all that is in me, and with the Lord's help."

Sam paused, then leaned forward slightly in her chair and lowered her voice to a near whisper. "Mrs. Foster, would you, could you, please consider selling me your home?"

It was not the way any university school of business worth its salt recommended such a financial proposal take place. This was not how things were done. But this was Freedom, and here, folks sometimes didn't get the memo on how others thought commerce should proceed. People here still believed in speaking their minds; that a handshake and an honest person's word were worth more than legal documents;

that roots mattered. Or at least that's what Sam supposed about her hometown.

Before she gave Sam an answer, June Foster felt she had to explain why she was selling the family home. There remained no direct-line Fosters to inherit it. She and her late husband, Frederick, had never had children. It needed work.

June didn't add that she was beyond living here physically, but that was more obvious now than either woman acknowledged. Before a health crisis, June wanted to make the move into one of the new assisted-living apartments that just opened west of town overlooking the Freedom Reservoir.

Like Sam, she was trying to take the bull by the horns and move on to her next chapter. Ironically, the two women had a lot in common. Both needed to make drastic changes in their lives. Mrs. Foster admired Sam's spunk and had seen that same quality before in Sam's father—and in herself. Honestly, most people in this town tiptoed around her, and she knew it. She admired someone brave enough to speak with her directly and so concisely.

Mrs. Foster told Sam about John Whetsel, the Foster family attorney for decades, and his colleague, town real-estate-agency owner Dan Frame, and how neither of them would be happy if she sold the place to Samantha.

Sam was astonished by June's candor. It was almost as though June had been waiting on her, anticipating some sort of intervention into the plans that were unfolding.

Each of those men, in fact, had privately tried to buy the house from June. They couldn't wait to get hold of the Foster place, and while the town matriarch knew it was time to sell, she dreaded all the chatter listing it would cause. Yet if she singled out one of those men to buy it, or sold it to anyone else in town, she would have to deal with the competitive squabbling that would surely be the talk of the town.

Better to just list it on the open market, she figured, and let the chips fall where they may. Still, she told Sam, this had all unsettled her something awful and had caused her to delay listing the place. She should have let it go before now, but dreaded the entire process.

At this stage of her life, June didn't want the fuss. Still, the thought of the looks on those men's oh-so-serious faces if she sold the house to someone else—someone outside of their expected cast of rivals; someone like Samantha Jones Jarrett—well, it nearly made her laugh aloud. She didn't mean it in a nasty way, but darn it, they were trying to tell her what to do with her own property, and she didn't like that one bit. Until the ink was dry on a change of deed, this house was still hers.

"Do they take me for an old fool?" June asked Sam. "I know good and well why both of those men want it. Dan wants it for his lady friend and John for his pet organization. Well, I'm leaving the community forum plenty, and Frederick's family has done more for it and this town, honestly, than anyone else in the history of Freedom. But as for this house, I am simply not keen on it no longer holding families."

If Whetsel bought it, Mrs. Foster, explained, he would turn around and sell it to his pride and joy, the United County Business and Cultural Forum, which would turn it into an elegant office building.

If Dan bought it, his Ellen Madison would move in immediately.

"It rubs me wrong the way these men call to inquire about my health; the way they both send flowers and candy and offer to take me for Sunday drives," Mrs. Foster unloaded. "Do they think I can't see right through their motives? Do they think that I don't know that they are merely lobbyists trying to get in good with me so I will sell them my property and leave this town my money? Phooey!"

June confided that there was something about Ellen that didn't sit well with her. "She does a fine job directing the marketing of Foster Foods, certainly, but she seems, well, always on the make for something bigger," June told Sam pointedly. "Something like my house." She said that Ellen was "too big for her own britches."

Mrs. Foster was not responsible for any personnel-management decisions at Foster Foods as that had all been turned over to a board of trustees and its staff before her husband even passed, so she didn't say anything and respected those in authority over the operations. But still. June could see right through Ellen's too-friendly overtures.

Ellen and June were both proud of their families' early links to the town of Freedom, but Ellen seemed to use the past, curiously, as a way to get an upper hand with people. It was more of an attitude than anything.

"I love the pioneer stories that surround the Fosters and the Madisons, but they are just that—old stories," June said. "The people who moved to town later are every bit as important and entitled to a say in Freedom business as those whose families have seemingly always been here. Ellen is boorish."

Mrs. Foster did not abide small-town arrogance and the way Ellen acted as though her family came over on the Mayflower and landed not on Plymouth Rock but pressed on to the banks of the Freedom Reservoir.

Sam was getting an education. Mrs. Foster went on.

If Ellen got her hands on June's home, it would be her biggest feat since she paid to move the historic Madison family chicken coop to the town park as a historical monument and then insisted that she ride as grand marshal of the Freedom Pioneer Day Parade to brag about it.

"Just because her family's chicken pen is the oldest surviving one known in the state, and she paid to rescue it, doesn't amount to a hill of beans," June said. "The thought is ridiculous; just the sort of thing people laugh about behind her back. Goodness to Pete, you'd think the woman founded the town herself because of that blasted chicken building."

Sam tried to take in all that she was hearing while at the same time, make the best pitch of her own for buying the house, and explain why she longed to return to Freedom.

"Samantha, dear, you have blindsided me with your proposal. Here I thought I would sign some papers and let the highest bidder take this old place. But I must say, your idea has put a wrinkle in my plan."

"I don't doubt that one bit, Mrs. Foster," Sam said. "And I thank you for hearing me out."

"Tell you what," June Foster said, eyes suddenly bright with an idea. "Why don't I have Joanie fix us a nice dinner, and why don't you spend the night? Yes, try out one of those rooms upstairs that you envision for guests. I need some thinking time."

Samantha knew a moment that she could not pass up when she saw one. "I would be honored," she said, and meant it. She freshened up in one of the upstairs bedrooms, the one with an ornate cherry-wood bed and antique sofa under the window that looked out over the Foster grounds and North Main Street. Then, she browsed around the upstairs library and selected a stack of magazines that she would relax with after dinner.

By then, Joanie called upstairs that dinner was ready. Mrs. Foster and Sam enjoyed Joanie's signature corn-and-chicken chowder, homemade bread, and more hot tea. They did not discuss the house or Samantha's offer. Instead, they talked about Herb Jones and local school days of another era. They spoke about what was new in Freedom and the positive impact the reservoir was having on the town. It was a pleasant meal, and once it was over, the two ladies retired to their separate quarters.

It had been a long, magical day. Samantha took a soak in the massive claw-foot bathtub and delved, mindlessly, into her reading material. She was emotionally and physically spent. She had given everything she had in her heart, and on her mind, in presenting her case to June Foster. It was all out of her hands now. As she stepped out of the tub, Samantha felt in her spirit some words of comfort: *It's going to be OK, Sam. Trust me.*

Indeed, she wanted to trust. It just didn't come easily these days.

Sleep, however, did come easily in that soft, warm bed.

⟲

SAMANTHA AWAKENED TO THE scent of coffee, quickly got dressed, and went downstairs. June Foster was already seated at the dining-room table. Joanie served them both coffee and asked Samantha how she took her eggs. As the main course was prepared, Mrs. Foster resumed the conversation they both knew was coming.

She told Samantha how much money she would need for her home. Sam nearly fainted when the figure was finally out in the open. But still, after selling her Green Hills house and cashing in some other securities, it was possible. Maybe not smart, even, but it could really happen.

"Samantha, I can see you are running the numbers as we speak. While it may seem a large sum, I want you to know that the quote I am giving you is considerably less than what I planned to list it for with the agency. But that information must remain between the two of us."

"Are you saying—" Sam asked.

"I am, indeed," Mrs. Foster said, smiling ear to ear.

"Samantha Ruth Jones Jarrett, you have just purchased my house."

With that, Sam let out her breath, and it sounded like a gust of wind sweeping through the dining room.

"I know you will take fine care of it. I could get more money from city folks. That blamed Dan Frame has been beating a path to my door for months with tales of how much that figure might be if I didn't first sell it to him, which is his preference. I don't care about that. What's money, anyway?" Mrs. Foster asked.

"I've got more than I need, and no one to leave it to but this community. The best thing I can do for this town, looks to me, is to see you keep this house up and share it with others. And besides, if it's a B and B, I can come and spend the night as I darn well please—as a *paying* customer, of course. It's the best of both worlds. That's how I see it. Now, would you like a coffee refill?"

Samantha's head ached from the tension. She had accomplished her goal, all right, but she also had just used up her savings to buy a big old house. Her entire life was about to completely change. She hadn't even sold her home in Green Hills. *What had she been thinking?*

To Freedom natives, this would still be called the old Foster place a hundred years from now. But to those who came from neighboring cities, or from out of state to stay here, to spend the night and be pampered in a small town with a big reservoir, it would not be the Foster place at all.

It would be United County's premiere bed-and-breakfast; never mind that it would be the county's *only* bed-and-breakfast.

It would be Sweetland.

Sweetland of Liberty Bed & Breakfast in Freedom, Indiana.

FOUR

Can't Be True

JOHN WHETSEL SLAMMED DOWN the phone and buzzed his assistant. "Hold my calls."

He couldn't figure this out. He'd been handling June Foster's affairs for, what, three decades now? Ever since he moved to town to take over the law firm of the late Glen Reynolds.

In all of his years in Freedom, he'd never once heard of this Samantha Jarrett. Evidently she was from here originally, and yes, he knew of her brother, Jim Jones, a decent fellow with a Christmas-tree farm outside of town, but Samantha? She seemed to have appeared out of nowhere. Where had she been all these years, and how in heaven's name had she talked June into this deal? What would bring her back now?

It was beyond him. And he didn't like it.

The attorney liked knowing everything there was to know about this town, and what was going on in it too. He was at the top of the heap as far as power and influence went around here, and he loved it. To think that someone, some—*woman*— could just waltz into Freedom and sweep out again the next day with the most prime piece of real estate to become available in years, well, she had another thing coming, indeed.

June called to tell him about the sale of her home to this woman, but she intentionally failed to give many details. The attorney got out of her that the purchase agreement was verbal at this point, and he was quick to point out that with nothing in writing, June could back out of the whole thing this minute and be perfectly within her legal rights. He must have come across too gruffly because June was offended by his comment.

"John Whetsel, my word is my oath. I have no thought whatsoever in going back on my agreement with Samantha. And not only that, but I have not the slightest desire to reverse this decision. I have plenty of money, John. Money is not everything in this world. Maybe someday you will see that for yourself. I believe that I am supposed to sell this place to her, and that is just what I am going to do—with or without your blessing. It matters not one bit to me."

John was skeptical, to say the least. A person doesn't just material-ize out of thin air, without any kind of warning, and talk someone as prominent as June Foster into selling her house. That is not how it is done. It's flat-out rude! The very *notion* of some random woman ap-proaching June in such a direct way.

There had to be more to it than appeared on the surface. Besides, June had expressed her plan to list her house for sale with Dan Frame. A date was set to do just that. What happened to June's promise about that, anyway? Where was her precious "word-is-my-oath" integrity? He'd be sure to mention *that* point, and he scribbled a note as such on his yellow legal pad.

What had this Jarrett woman promised June, anyway? And what could she have possibly said that got her inside the door of the Foster house, first past June's long-time gatekeeper and housekeeper-cook Joanie, and second, to broach the topic of buying such an elite historic residence?

Frankly, he was appalled at the nerve of this Jarrett woman. He didn't know her personally, but he knew enough about her already to be entirely certain of one thing: he did not like her, and he never would.

She would never be accepted in this town if he had anything to do with it. And he would make it his personal business to see to it, besides.

The timing was highly questionable too. How could this Jarrett woman have known that the house would be going up for sale? There must be a snitch in this office, that's it, or in Dan's. Or maybe it had something to do with Jarrett's brother. How would Jones have access to such confidential information as the listing of June's home?

Whetsel would have to get to the bottom of this, and do it quickly. He would find out who was feeding Samantha Jarrett details about this town. She couldn't possibly have just woken up one day and decided to buy a house in another state. No one does that.

Hatching a sneaky plan like that took, well, years. He would know.

The attorney was not in a good mood. In fact, he was just plain mad, and getting angrier by the minute.

As president of the United County Business and Cultural Forum, he had long planned on delivering June's house safely into the organization's hands, locating the forum office there, and turning the old homestead into an elegant community-gathering space. He had spent considerable time thinking this thing through; not to mention catering to June's every whim.

Why, he bought her more flowers and took her on more scenic rides looking at *cornfields* and even purchased more blamed tickets for her bus trips to dinner theaters than he ever thought of doing for his own wife. And this is how he is thanked? By June yanking the property right out from under him and selling it to some newcomer? He was so close to getting it too.

For years, John had dreamed of just how fine his own law office would look, relocated in that left parlor of hers and in the rooms behind it.

Next, the economic-development office could be in there, right across the foyer from his private law firm. After some remodeling, the main floor would provide a wonderful conference room for officials to meet and greet prospective business-and-industry leaders who were thinking of locating in town.

He could see it all now: The old house would be the town's welcome center for all of the movers and shakers who thought about making Freedom a part of their business-and-industry expansion plans. It would be for the good of the entire town; a community service, in fact. Yes, he would be doing everyone in town a favor by landing that old house, and getting the forum to write some kind of grant to foot the bill for the whole works.

Maybe they should add a tourism center; display museum arti-
facts—even put Ellen's blasted chicken coop in the backyard. And just
why not? There was no limit to the possibilities.

And with his law firm front and center of it all, he wouldn't miss a
beat. Every move anyone who counted in this town made would take
place right outside his door, if not inside it. This kind of power and control were what he had been working toward his entire career.

Truth be told, he half expected June to surprise everyone at the
last minute and donate the house to the forum for the general good of
United County. It made fine sense. There were no remaining Foster de-
scendants to leave her money to, so why not gift the house for the ben-
efit of all?

Some nights he couldn't sleep just thinking about what could be.

Why, besides letting him move his law office there, the forum board
would probably insist on a plaque with his name on it, and possibly his
likeness as well, engraved, bronzed, and hung there in the foyer in rec-
ognition for all of his considerable effort in pulling this project together,
for his uncanny vision. It would be only right to accept it too given that
he had gone to so much trouble to secure the property—for the common
good, of course. But if they suggested a life-size statue on the lawn, well,
he'd have to draw the line at that one. He was nothing, if not a modest
man.

He'd hinted around for years about his idea of June donating the
property, but she wouldn't make that commitment. It didn't matter
now, John thought, frustrated. All of the plans were for nothing. As of
today, apparently this deal was done.

Funny, but he always perceived that his greatest rival in acquiring
the Foster place was his colleague Dan Frame, who ran the only real-
estate business in town, and who was on the zoning board. They used
to joke privately on the way to forum meetings: "You know, buddy,"
one would say to the other, "the day will come when one of us is happy
about the Foster house and the other—not so much."

They promised each other that no matter what came of it, they
would both survive and remain on good terms both personally and

professionally. Neither of them was going anywhere, so they had to get along. Or at least have the appearance of civility.

Darn it! How could this whole thing be falling through?

Dan would not be happy, either.

But worse still, Dan's long-time companion, Ellen, would fairly combust. She fancied herself as a friend of June's. She directed the marketing division of Foster Foods of Freedom and as such spent much of her time out promoting the brand all over the region, and beyond.

In fact, she was away from Freedom at trade shows and showcases about as much as she was in town.

◡◠

JUST LIKE JOHN, ELLEN truly thought she had the inside track on the sale of the Foster place. After all, June and her late husband were the last of the Fosters, and since Ellen had devoted her career to working for their business complex, she thought she had settled herself into June's good graces. Ellen wielded her long-time marketing expertise at Foster Foods, used her silver tongue on June at every opportunity possible, and perhaps of more value, promoted her own pioneer heritage to the hilt.

The Fosters were all about history. They *were* history in this town. Among other things, the family started the United County Historical Society. Ellen made it a point never to miss a meeting. She wanted to be front and center every time June was around. "After all, the town's few blue bloods have to stick together," she whispered to anyone of a like mind.

Ellen even kidded Dan that maybe he wouldn't have to finagle June into a residential-home sales contract after all because June just might up and give her the place free and clear.

"And why not?" Ellen asked him. "With no Fosters waiting in the wings, I plan to be June's surrogate daughter, of sorts. Of course I'll see to it that the mansion is maintained, and proudly preserve the Foster name just as I have kept the Madison heritage alive. I'm the only logical person to inherit, well, to live in anyway, the Foster home."

June Foster just might give her the keys to the castle, so to speak. And when she did, Ellen would take them and never look back.

Whetsel got a chill down his spine just thinking of all of that and how Ellen would react when she heard the news.

"And Daniel," Ellen joked once when the Whetsels were out to dinner with them, "I won't even need you anymore. I could write my own ticket for anything I want."

And she wanted a lot.

Ellen was at some business conference in New York City. Maybe Whetsel should break the news to Dan before her return. Give the guy a chance to figure out how to tell her. It would not be pretty.

Ellen Madison was more than a strong personality. She was a force of nature. And she did not take disappointment well. Come to think of it, had she ever even been disappointed before? John didn't want to think too long about the answer to that question.

The attorney's thinking was interrupted when he heard three crisp taps on his office door. "What?" he demanded.

His assistant, Kathy, cracked the door open and peeked inside. "I am so very sorry to bother you, Mr. Whetsel, but Mr. Frame is here to see you. I told him that you are not entertaining clients, but he insists that he must see you due to an urgent matter."

"Well, send him in, then," Whetsel barked.

Into the room burst Dan.

"John, what is this I hear about June selling her place to an outsider? I don't understand."

"Dan, I know. I'm as confused as the next person. June just called me herself to set up the legalities. When I told her to think it over and then we'd discuss it, she cut me off. Said she had done all of her thinking already, and the matter was closed. She is selling the house to Samantha Jarrett and that is that. She got awfully cranky with me."

Dan was on the edge of his leather seat in front of John's desk. "She told me the same thing; called me just before I walked over here. What can we do to turn this deal around?"

Whetsel said that he had talked to June until he was blue in the face about rethinking her decision but that it was over; there was to be no more discussion.

"In fact, Dan, she got downright short with me. Told me that if I took 'that tone' with her again and tried to tell her what to do with her house, she planned to tell me what I could do, and find herself another lawyer! Can you even imagine that?"

The two men spent the better part of the day trying to figure out their next move.

But it was Dan who had an even tougher assignment.

He had to tell Ellen.

FIVE

"I Want That House..."

DAN HAD TO TELL her, that's all there was to it. If he waited until Ellen got home from the business trip and then gave her the news, it would be much worse on both of them. He should ease the blow now, and get on with it. Besides, maybe she would calm herself down before he had to see her face-to-face.

The trouble was that Ellen had an elaborate plan for landing the Foster house. She had, in fact, started packing up some of her belongings in anticipation. She was that certain that her plan would come to pass and she would be moving before summer. Now her scheme was useless. And he was the one who had to tell her.

Dan had been given clear instructions from his beloved to buy the house, whatever the cost, as soon as June signed the listing. He was to jump in and offer full asking price before John Whetsel could make his move.

Ellen figured that John would try to be smooth about it, and want to meet Dan for coffee and discuss proceeding before getting around to coughing up the money. Whetsel didn't think that Dan would just go ahead and make the offer on the spot. It wasn't his style.

But Dan and Ellen planned to pull a fast one on the attorney. Ellen cautioned Dan not to permit June to leave the office before he bought the house outright and signed the papers. Then, he was to place a for-sale sign in June's front lawn that night, tell her it was a formality, and in a week or so, add SOLD across it so that everything seemed routine.

Freedom residents would just drive by and murmur to themselves, "Boy, that sale sure happened fast."

Ellen didn't care that John Whetsel would be insulted by Dan's fast moves. All three of them had been jockeying for position for a very long time. Since June had decided to put it on the open market, if word got out, someone else could buy it first. The plan was not to give Whetsel, or anyone else, that opportunity. They weren't going to talk this deal to death and let the house get away from them or let the attorney move in for the kill after pleading his case to Dan about why he should be the one to buy it.

Ellen didn't want any glitches.

The SOLD sign would remain on the front lawn for a few weeks, and then disappear. Life would go on as usual for the people of Freedom, and it would be wonderful for Ellen and Dan.

Besides all that, she held out the hope that maybe June would gift the house to her, after all.

Big changes generally came slowly in this town. Or at least slow enough that people could talk about something forever before something really, if ever, happened. This was so annoying to Ellen. Traveling like she did, she saw that people elsewhere simply took action. City people didn't blab endlessly about dreams that would never happen. They made their dreams come true. And she would too.

Never mind that the Fosters had owned the place more than two centuries. All that the fine folks of Freedom would know is that the stately home had always been there, then a for-sale sign went up, and then new owners with local pedigrees took possession.

Ellen had the pedigree. Now all she needed was possession: a minor detail, in her mind.

Then, when a fair amount of time had passed, the real plan would take shape.

Dan and Ellen would resell the home to Kim and Vance Brayton, a married pair of entrepreneurs from New York City. This time, it would be a very quiet transaction *without* a for-sale sign. Locals probably wouldn't even realize that anyone other than Dan and Ellen were the owners.

The Braytons were fabulously wealthy. Ellen had gotten acquainted with them at one of the food trade shows she attended out east several years ago on a Foster Foods business trip. The Braytons were in the warehouse-food business, only on a national scale. Ellen and Kim had instantly hit it off and kept company with each other through the years at trade shows.

Kim Brayton's passion was decorating her family's multiple homes, and she furnished two of the ones they owned around the country with items handcrafted in the Midwest. Kim had grown up on the East Coast and was for some reason fascinated by the fly-over states. She'd never spent time in the corn belt, but she enjoyed hearing Ellen's stories about the laid-back, rural culture of Freedom. It seemed so wholesome to Kim compared to the city life with which she was far more acquainted.

The two women spent many evenings at conferences talking about the small Indiana town where Ellen lived, and its country lifestyle. Kim romanticized Ellen's life to the point where she talked her husband into visiting this town that sounded so charming.

After much prodding by Ellen, the Braytons decided it would be a lark to add an authentic midwestern house to their inventory if—and it was a big if—they found one that struck their fancy. When they visited Freedom, they drove around until they handpicked the exact one they wanted. It didn't take them long to locate it, either: it was the Foster place.

"That particular house might be difficult to purchase," Ellen had said, explaining.

"That's nice, Ellen, but that's the house I want," Kim said flatly. "I've heard that story before and it only makes me want a property more. Look, I really don't care what it costs. New York, California prices. It doesn't matter. Just get it for me."

Since it would be just one of several homes that they owned, they would only be in Freedom for a few weeks each summer. "You and Dan can even live there all but those three or so weeks," Kim told Ellen. "Enjoy the place and make sure everything is in order is all I ask. You can be the caretakers. We'll even pick up the utilities."

Ellen was amazed by the offer.

"So are you in?" Kim asked her.

"You had better believe that I am!" Ellen responded. "That *we* are. We are *so* in." Ellen never wanted anything more in her entire life.

Dan and Ellen would make a killing off of Mrs. Foster by buying the house for whatever amount she wanted and then more than at least double the price when they sold it to the Braytons. And, besides, they would get to live there, completely free. People might wonder how they pulled it off, but they would not discuss the details of the special arrangement. It would be their little mystery for the gossip mill, and best of all, it was all perfectly legal. It was free enterprise.

Then during the few weeks each summer that the Braytons were in Freedom, no doubt bringing along their wealthy city friends for boating on the reservoir, Ellen and Dan would leave town, taking their own vacations elsewhere. They would be able to afford trips to virtually anywhere on the planet since they would not have housing expenses and would have all of the profits stashed away from their sale to the Braytons. It was perfect! It was also their ticket to living the kind of routine lavish lifestyle that Ellen always dreamed about, and eventually, to retirement security as well. And they would do so right under everyone's noses.

∽

"ELLEN, PLEASE CALL ME," Dan spoke in a serious tone into her voice mail.

To himself, Dan practiced phrasing and rephrasing his choice of words. What could he possibly say to keep Ellen from exploding? There was no sugarcoating anything, try as he might. The Jarrett woman had bought the place, and that was that. June wouldn't release how much the buyer paid for it, either. She had become a stone wall to his and John's inquiries.

After all of the time and trouble they had gone to, competing with each other for her house, it came down to June selling the thing on a whim to an outsider. Who could have ever seen that coming? It was irresponsible of her, to say the least, and Ellen wouldn't be able to accept it. He was certain of that.

"Danny!" Ellen beamed, returning his call. She certainly was in a good mood. "So what's up, my main man?"

"Ellen, honey, I hope you are somewhere that you can talk. I'm afraid I have some bad news for you. You'll want to sit down."

"Is everyone all right?"

"Yes, it's not that. But Ellen, honey, I don't know how to put this to you gently, so I'll just say it."

"Daniel, you are scaring me. Stop it. What is going on?"

"Sweetheart," Dan started, "we've lost the Foster house."

Silence.

"What did you say?"

"I know. It's hard to take, my love" Dan said. "Some woman from Ohio bought it out from under us. She plans to move here as soon as possible and open an inn. It's over, Ellen. We'll just have to find another dream, another house. Another one will come on the market. You'll see."

"No, Daniel, I won't see," Ellen said. "This can't be. You know the plans I've had for that place—that was our retirement, our ticket to living the good life right there in Freedom. Our future, Daniel. No! I will not be denied that house. Kim Brayton told me if I didn't get her June's place they didn't want any other one around town. She loves that house, and it is her first and only choice. The deal will be over if we can't deliver. It's that serious, Daniel."

"Well, what can I do?" Dan pleaded. "John says it's for real."

"I can call June. She'll listen to me. I have devoted my life to her family's company, and Daniel, you know how our families date back to the start of the town. Surely she would rather that I get it than some nobody," Ellen said, her words coming out faster and faster. "That's it. She just doesn't realize that I want it this much. I can change her mind. I know I can."

"Ellen, June is angry that we are challenging her decision. John and I have both tried. She won't even take our calls now. She likes this woman who bought it. She went to school with her father or something. I honestly don't think there is one thing we can do," he said. "I tried.

I really tried before calling you. John and I both did. If there was any other way—"

"Just hold it right there, you spineless wimp," Ellen interrupted. "Back it up a minute and explain this to me from the beginning. What I want to know is why now? Why just weeks before we had it in the bag? This does not make any sense, Daniel, and I hold you responsible. How could you let this happen? Didn't you know there was someone sniffing around the property? What's her name, this woman?"

"Samantha Jarrett."

"I don't know any Samantha Jarrett," Ellen barked. "Who is she? Why is she coming to town?"

"Apparently her maiden name is Jones, and she's originally from here. She'd be about your age, I guess, from what June said."

Silence. Ellen was thinking.

"Oh. My. Gosh," Ellen said, suddenly making a connection. "Samantha Jones. Yes, I remember that little goody-two-shoes. We did go to school together. I never liked her at all, either. Yep, knew her as kids and then she went away to college, got married to some guy from somewhere else, I think. But why? How? Why now?"

"I don't know, dear. When you get—"

Ellen interrupted him with a burst of anger. "Don't you dare 'dear' me, Daniel. I don't know or care why this woman bought my house, but I will tell you this, and you would be wise to listen carefully. No one does this to me. Is that clear to you, Daniel Frame? Certainly not Miss Country Bumpkin Samantha Jones Whatever! How dare she come into this town and rip my house right out from under me when I was just weeks in sight of our dream? I will get that house, Daniel. Am I making myself even remotely clear? That house will be mine. You mark my words. And Samantha Jones had better mark them too."

And with that, the phone went silent.

It was Dan who had to sit down.

SIX

Risky Business

WHAT HAD SHE DONE...

Just like that, Sam purchased her dream house, alone, without Roger. Without anyone's blessing or promise of sweat equity, either. Mrs. Foster was drawing up the papers, and they'd finalize it all in a couple of weeks. It was a lot to take in. What Sam felt was the oddest mixture of buyer's remorse and euphoria.

As she drove northeast from Freedom, Sam's mind was racing, and her hands were sweating. She had a long drive and more to think about than she could mentally compartmentalize.

She had just bought a new life, to the extent that one can do that, but had plenty of the old one left to deal with too. She was still employed at the college for a few weeks. She had a house to pack up and sell. There would be lots of tearful good-byes to friends in Green Hills. It would be harder to leave her gal pals than she could even imagine. There was the move. And what then? It would take a strong marketing plan to get people to actually *stay* at her new inn. She prayed for strength and guidance; endurance too.

She called Gus first. "I have some big news," Sam led off, trying to sound her most positive.

"Hey, Mama. And what would that be on this cold winter's day?"

"Are you sitting down?"

Gus laughed. "No, but hit me with it anyway."

After she explained the sequence of the past few days' activities, Gus was both surprised and excited for her. "Mom, that is amazing. I never knew that you and Dad thought about doing this. I think it's great. Shake things up; start over again. Why the heck not? You're just fifty."

"Well, I don't think your brother will see it quite that way, but I sure do appreciate your support, Gus."

"You've got to live your life, Mom. I've been telling you that all along. I can see this working for you. I really can. I'm proud of you for taking a chance."

They talked for a good twenty-mile chunk of her drive north. Then she called Ray. This conversation wasn't going to be easy like the one with Gus.

"Honey, I've got some news," Sam started. "I think you'll be surprised."

She went through the whole saga again, only this time with a different reaction from her older son.

"I just don't know, Mom," Ray said, sounding increasingly disturbed with each word. "When did you do this? Who up and buys an ancient house in an old town, alone? Why didn't you discuss this with me first? You are fifty, for heaven's sake. That's not exactly young." Ray was not pleased. It wasn't long before he had to go. He always had to go.

Sam didn't know what she expected to hear from her sons. At least one was encouraging. Sam arrived home after dark. She had to face Joanna first thing in the morning and would need her energy. She didn't unpack or even go through her mail. She just went to bed.

⁓

THE NEXT MORNING, SAM got to work on time and walked straight into her boss's office. "I need to speak with you, Joanna," Sam said, sitting down directly in front of the president without first being asked.

"What have you been up to, Sam?" Joanna inquired. "What has *mysteriously* kept you so busy for two days during this frantic time here at work?"

"Joanna, I'm afraid that I have some big news this week. You see, you won't believe this, but I drove to my hometown in Indiana to check into buying a house that I have loved all of my life. Roger and I had discussed purchasing it and turning it into a bed-and-breakfast. After everything that happened last week, it occurred to me that this might be the ideal—the only—time, in fact, to make this happen. What do you think?" Sam sat back and smiled.

Joanna sipped her morning coffee and said nothing.

"So, I did it. I bought the house," Sam added, filling the silence. "It all happened so fast. It all is *still* happening so fast. I plan to support myself there in the years to come. It's a complete lifestyle change, and it is scary, but I have to tell you—I'm really excited. I will need to take quite a few personal days in the coming weeks. There's a good chance I'll be leaving this job before you even retire."

"I see," Joanna said, looking agitated by the news. "I must say, Sam, I thought you had better sense than to run off and do something so impulsive. I have to question your judgment."

Sam felt the heat rise on her neck. This was not the response she expected. Not only did she fail to get a warm congratulations, she was getting quite the opposite, and a good scolding besides.

Joanna picked up steam. "Frankly, this is about the silliest plan I could ever imagine. Haven't you ever heard that you can't go home again?" Joanna asked. "Those people who live in those tiny dots on the map are narrow-minded, Samantha. What makes you think they will welcome you back? You've changed a great deal in the three decades since you lived there. They might just run you out of that little town on a rail! What were you thinking? Whatever it was, spare me the details. I've got to get to work."

"Joanna—what is wrong with you? I thought you of anyone would be supportive of my idea to try something completely new and different. Yes, it's a risk. But what in life isn't risky? What do I have to lose? I am soon without a job. I'm a widow for heaven's sa—"

The president cut Sam off. "Stop right there. I've heard enough about this. Are you finished?"

"As a matter of fact, I am, Joanna. I am *quite finished,*" Sam told her boss. "It was bad enough that you didn't respect me enough to tell me ahead of every John and Jane Doe on campus that you are leaving; that my job is ending. Bad enough that you continued to treat me so abruptly and not even think for one moment about my well-being. But now, you are also insulting my hometown and my dream, and I won't tolerate it. I'm done, Joanna. Have a nice life."

Sam didn't even bother to gather her personal things from her desk, or stop by human resources to sign any papers. She simply walked out the door, took the stairs to the main floor, and then drove off campus toward Green Hills.

She had some packing to do.

SEVEN

Nowhere Else to Go

SAMANTHA DIDN'T SLOW DOWN for a week after the movers deposited all of her worldly belongings inside the old house—her new home—in Freedom.

Once they unloaded everything on moving day, she, Sally, and Ray got busy filling dresser drawers, making beds, and unpacking the kitchen. Sam giggled to herself when Ray spread out her baking pans single file, flat, in the pantry where the food should go. No two people ever arranged a kitchen the same way. But it didn't matter. She was just glad to have her kids there. The belongings could all be moved around later.

She was a Freedom resident for a week already, and while the pantry was now rearranged the way she wanted it, there was plenty in the house, and in her life, that was not.

Although Sam longed to visit with her family members during moving weekend, and process everything that had happened in such a brief period of time, as well as catch up on what was new with them, Ray was not in the mood for reflection. He was truly more angry with than he was happy for his mother; she could sense it, and neither of them had much to say to each other.

He didn't like worrying about what she was up to, and this was a venture he certainly didn't understand. He thought she was having a midlife crisis, surely a latent reaction to his father's death.

Sam could always see right through her older son. It was as though she knew exactly what Ray was thinking: *Why couldn't she just buy a country-club membership and take up golf, or volunteer in a soup kitchen? Did she really have to uproot her entire life? Couldn't she and her friends keep busy shopping, or whatever it is that they do together?*

One thing was for sure: Ray didn't want to be dragged into this mess.

And to him, it sure felt like a mess, all right.

❧

"IT COULD BE," SALLY suggested privately, to her husband, "that your mother is losing her mind. Seriously, I read an article about early-onset Alzheimer's disease. It could explain things. This is the time in life where she should be scaling back, not making her life—and ours, and your brother's, really—more complex."

"I know that losing her job is a setback," Ray told his wife. "She's been through a lot. But why is she over-reacting with a jump off the deep end? What does she know about running a business, anyway? None of it makes sense."

He questioned his mother. "Can't you just ask the college to reassign you to the media-relations department or something?" But it was too late now.

She had a communications degree and had worked in corporate relations in downtown Cleveland for a while before joining the college staff and then moving into her current position. Before those jobs, she stayed home with the boys when they were small. Exasperation rose on the edge of Ray's voice.

Sam thought maybe she *could have* taken her son's suggestion about a reassignment.

Maybe she even should have.

"I probably could eventually find another campus job. Or something downtown," Sam told Ray. "But it's not easy anymore. I'd be competing with all of those driven, tech-savvy twenty-five-year-olds with boundless energy set on one speed: FAST! Besides, with you, Sally, and Gus living so far away, this seems like the time to try something different—something that uses skills that I most enjoy like decorating, cooking, baking, volunteering in the town. And, I could use a complete change of scenery. I think this is it. At least I'm banking on it, literally."

Ray listened but didn't have a verbal response; just a frown.

Gus couldn't get away for the big move. He promised to visit later when the dust settled. Sam looked forward to that because of his cheerful view on everything going on in her life.

"Don't fret about Ray, or about any of it. Mom, I say if this is what you want, go for it," Gus told her. These were words that she craved hearing right about now. His view was in the minority among the people in her life.

Once June Foster gave the green light to buying Sweetland, everything happened far quicker than Sam imagined possible. Her Green Hills house sold immediately—without a real-estate agency, even, when a friend's daughter got wind that Sam was planning to move and made an offer to buy it. It wasn't full asking price but was close enough so that Sam could accept it and get on with her life.

But the happy news she planned to share was short-lived. Everyone besides Gus, it seemed, thought she was nuts. Her banker and investment counselor both begged her to reconsider. They couldn't make the figures work to their liking. She was buying an expensive property with no data available to support any real expectation for recovering her investment. It was beyond a risky-business deal. Only intuition told her she was doing the right thing.

Her close friends were floored when she called them. The conversation was not about their usual favorite topics, but rather to say that she was leaving them. They didn't know what to make of her plans. They never even knew before now that she considered opening a bed-and-breakfast, and this new information, coming after she bought one, made them feel left out.

Even her brother Jim, and his wife Jenny, had little to offer when Sam told them the good news that she would be living just blocks away from them in Freedom and back in everyone's lives again. This wasn't the Sam they all knew. They guessed that being a widow does strange things to a woman.

⁊⁊

BEFORE ROGER DIED, SAM had no idea that widowhood was a subculture all its own. Then she found out.

Roger wasn't gone a month when she was approached on campus one afternoon by a pleasant professor she knew casually. He asked her to join him for coffee. Thinking that it was surely about educational matters, she agreed. But all he wanted to talk about was his late wife, and how wonderful she had been, and how lonely he was. He didn't give Sam a chance to even mention Roger, just droned on about Margaret, and the loss he was feeling.

Sam thought maybe he just needed an empathetic ear, so she listened and nodded through one large coffee, black; one refill, with cream; and at least two glances at her watch before she finally told the colleague that she needed to go.

But instead of thanking her for her understanding, he said that since both of them were lonely, they could help each other out. Sam was a bit dense at first about what he meant by that, but her face was surely red when he went on to suggest that they go back to his place for a couple of hours to "work out the grief."

He clearly had no interest in discussing their careers, or Roger, with her. She excused herself gracefully. He thought she was visiting the ladies' room, but instead, she bolted out the side door and nearly ran across campus to the familiar safety of her office, her heart pounding.

One evening not long after that, she answered the doorbell to find a neighbor from around the block, an old golfing buddy of Roger's actually, standing there smiling broadly, holding a large vase of flowers. She recognized the pink roses from his wife's garden as the woman was often busy in it when Sam drove home from work. Sam accepted the fragrant flowers and told him to be sure to thank his wife for her.

"These are not from the wife; they are from me, alone," he said too softly. She quickly told him to leave, shoving the floral arrangement firmly into his chest as he left.

She mentally relived the disgusting incident nearly daily in the summer months as the man's wife smiled and waved from her rose garden when Sam drove by their property. If only there had been a different route home, she would have taken it. The poor neighbor woman was clueless.

Sam thought of old stereotypes about widows being easy prey for men who perceived them as lonely and weak, but the thought of cozying up to any man—let alone a married one, or one still in love with his dead wife—was the last thing on her mind.

Then that fall, Tonya, a widowed friend from church who was several years older than Sam, insisted that they attend an open house at the new senior-condo complex where Tonya had just purchased a residence. Tonya was excited about her move, and Sam was happy for her. It would be refreshing to be around someone who was upbeat despite her own far-from-ideal life circumstances. Why not? She thought she would go to the open house and check it out.

Sam had always enjoyed Tonya's vibrant personality when they occasionally worked together on church committees, but they weren't really close. Now, the friend decided that since they were both on the younger side of widowhood, they should get to know each other better.

Maybe it was a good idea; Tonya seemed to understand when Sam explained what had happened with the two men hitting on her. She'd experienced a similar incident. It was good to have a perspective from someone who had been there.

It was probably smart to befriend another widow, anyway. Sam didn't think she could talk to her best friends, or to her kids, about such things. It could be that spending more time with Tonya, and maybe even joining her widows' support group, would be good ideas.

Then came the Greener Pastures Retirement Village Open House.

"Sam, I just know you would love it out here," Tonya beamed as though she was selling on commission. "Life is so full! We play bingo Monday nights. Tuesdays are crafts, and the second Wednesdays of the month we bake birthday cakes in the community room and share them on the second Thursdays with those who want to celebrate their birthdays. I tell you, Sam, there's more to do here than you can get done."

The woman was a human calendar as she rattled off one activity after the next, each one preplanned, and neatly inked inside the condo complex's monthly newsletter. All the residents had to do was show up.

Tonya said she was saving the best activity for last. She just knew this one would be perfect for Sam. It was none other than a residents' chapter of the True-Blue Scarf Club, whereby all of the ladies in the complex—most of them widows—sported blue scarves, coordinating handbags and shoes, and got together monthly to go shopping and out to eat.

"You'd love it, Sam! We don't even have to drive. We just load up the Greener Pastures bus, driver provided, and off we go. I'm telling you, it's a whole new lifestyle out here. You won't have to think about a thing. They've got everything covered for us."

Sam had a growing uneasy feeling about the complex. She didn't want everything on her calendar preplanned and figured out. She liked thinking about how to spend her own time and not going by a set calendar that someone else put together. She was perfectly capable of driving herself and her friends shopping anywhere they wanted. Celebrating the birthdays of strangers didn't interest her, and weekly bingo seemed like a waste of time.

Tonya was giving Sam a heavy sales pitch for buying the condo that was available next to her. They could do everything together, the friend said. "You'll have to get rid of half of everything in your house, but who needs all that stuff anyway?"

Sam listened, but the more Tonya said, the more she knew that there was no way under heaven that she would live at Greener Pastures at age fifty or sixty, or probably even seventy, either. All of a sudden Tonya seemed like a woman a full generation older. Sam thought the complex sounded wonderful for those who were ready to give up their traditional homes, and who were prepared for this step. But she knew one thing: She wasn't one of them. Not by a long shot. The idea depressed her.

Sam knew of no one her age who considered this step. *At least no one who was married.* Is this what being a widow—of any age—meant? This all made her feel even older.

"I'll have to give it some thought," Sam told her friend, not wanting to hurt her feelings, but now knowing full well that they really didn't have much in common, after all.

That night, as Sam walked through her house, she started considering what giving away half of everything might look like. *Let's see*, she wondered, rifling through her kitchen junk drawer. *Will it be adios to the turkey baster, or the nutcracker?* And in her bedroom closet, she looked at her scarf collection. *Should I keep the extra-long beige-and-white one that twists neatly into a knot at my throat, or the silky blue one that would—*Sam stopped in her thoughts—*be perfect for the True-Blue Scarf Club?*

She immediately took the perfectly good accessory and stuffed it into the trash. A sudden burst of anger filled her chest. She hated that she was feeling this way, and hated being a widow. She hated that scarf too and all that it represented.

There was no sense putting it off. She picked up the phone and called Tonya. She told her that she wasn't ready to make any decisions about moving into a condo, and didn't think she would even entertain those thoughts anytime in the foreseeable future.

After that, Tonya didn't call Sam again, and Sam didn't mind. They avoided each other at church. It was awkward. It seemed that the role of widow had its own landmines about which one who was married never gave a thought.

Aside from missing Roger, worrying about finances, and having friends and family who didn't understand what she was going through, Sam found that just because another woman was a widow didn't mean the two of them were on the same page.

Sam was nowhere near retirement. Even if finances allowed it, and they didn't, she wasn't ready to stop filling her own calendar and take up gated-community games. She wanted to make her own decisions, have her own belongings, make a difference in her own way. She wanted Sweetland of Liberty to succeed.

Sweetland was more than a new job. It represented something entirely fresh in her life: a new season, and probably her last chance to return to where she started. It was time that she saw what life had in store for her by living it her way rather than the way others thought she should. She was flying by the seat of her pants for the first time ever, and mostly, lately, it felt good.

ᥩᦧ

SAM AND ROGER MET while both were students at Frankfort College. They were in the library parking lot one fall day when Sam noticed that Roger's license plate was from the Hoosier state. She seldom ran into students from Indiana in northern Ohio. But more to the point, Roger was awfully cute, wherever he was from. So as they both were walking toward the library, she struck up a conversation, they chatted their way into the building, and went for coffee later that evening. They had been together ever since.

They graduated two and a half years after that first meeting, Roger with a business degree, and Sam with the communications diploma. That summer, they were married and lived for a while in one of her family's small rental houses in Freedom. Roger worked in the next city over. Then Ray was born. Soon after, Roger was given a promotion. The catch was, it required a transfer to Columbus, Ohio, and then, a few years later, another promotion took them back to the Cleveland area, where they had originally met. They had lived there ever since, establishing careers, and raising their family. Then, before they knew it, the boys were grown.

It would be selfish, and unrealistic, to think their sons would settle in the greater Cleveland area where they grew up. Sam certainly didn't stay in Freedom where she was raised, and the world had only gotten more expansive in opportunities and interconnected in technological advances since then. If opportunity beckoned elsewhere, most people nowadays no longer chose to remain in their hometowns.

The boys had to chart their own courses, and right now, their discoveries centered on St. Louis and Denver—not Green Hills, Ohio, and certainly not Freedom, Indiana, population three thousand—give or take a birth or an obituary.

It was impossible for the naysayers to process why Sam's future meant returning to her past. They couldn't see the old town through the eyes of her youth in any way.

Ray was especially blunt. "I just don't know why anyone would want to live in that little town, frankly. I have to wonder if a reservoir is enough incentive to bring in tourists. And would those people really be interested in staying in a B and B? Aren't they more of a camping crowd?"

Ray was sure that she had not researched this move, or thought it out well enough. "Where are the statistics to support a thing like this? And what about resale of an old house like that? Could you get back out of that place what you are putting into it?"

Sam didn't have the answers or statistics that Ray wanted. Every time they broached the subject, she was left feeling uninformed, and more than a little foolish.

The past was so present for Sam in this town. Memories surrounded her everywhere she went. The first night Ray and Sally were there, Sam took them to the local fast-food hangout, Roy Lee's. They ordered Hoosier tenderloin sandwiches and the house specialty, seasoned, crunchy potatoes. It was high school all over again for Sam. But the meal was not on Sally's diet and she was not impressed. To Ray, it was simply greasy fast food. *So much for a sentimental journey,* Sam thought. *What was I thinking bringing them here?* She so wished she hadn't.

For dessert, they enjoyed Mom's Spice Cake, gifted from the neighbor lady, Sue Conner, who dropped it off at the house. "Sue, this treat is a trip down memory lane," Sam told her neighbor. "My mom used to make an old-time cake just like it for special occasions. The scent of it takes me back to childhood, Christmas, Easter, and family reunions, all rolled into one dish."

Sam knew exactly what her new neighbor had in mind with the gesture. It was a brilliant, small-town method of gathering the latest news: Bake something wonderful and personally deliver it on occasions both happy and sad. If you are lucky enough to be invited inside the recipient's home, the take-away is always information. And be sure the homemade food is gifted in a pretty glass dish that needs to be returned, complete with the owner's name-and-address sticker on the bottom of the plate. That will ensure a second visit, and an update on the news you learned from the first one.

It's what people liked, yes—and disliked too—about small towns. Folks knew their neighbors all right, but sometimes they knew too much, and that knowledge could seem intrusive. Still, Sam was amazed by Sue's choice of desserts. Of all the options, she selected such a personal, sentimental favorite.

How could she have known that it would hit the spot?

⁓

SAM KNEW THAT PEOPLE were indeed interested in what was going on at her address. The cars slowed to a near stop as they passed. Gawkers tried to get glimpses inside the Foster place as they went for early-morning or evening walks. She had been gone a long time. Most folks didn't remember her. Many had moved to Freedom later, or were born there after she left. People wanted to see her, though, and figure out who she was, and how or if she fit into this town. Buying the Foster place was big stuff in Freedom.

But she didn't want to generate much attention just yet. Sam preferred getting the house in order first. And to accomplish that, there was a lot to do involving paint chips and repairmen. Only when she was ready to open would she install a tasteful, small sign in the front lawn.

Once the house had been refurbished and decorated to her satisfaction, Sam would walk the two blocks away and speak to *The United Times* editor about an article. Whether he would consider it news or not, and she figured he would, Sam would purchase a full-page advertisement to announce the open house.

She had to smile just thinking of the stir it would cause. No one took out full-page ads in the town's weekly paper. It was over the top. And it would get them all talking. She knew this about Freedom: everyone complained about *The Times*, but come each Wednesday morning, the publication was read cover to cover, and by noon, everyone was talking about who got arrested, who hosted the literary club, whose kid led the scoring on the basketball team, and how much pork chops were on sale for at Gil's Grocery.

With all of the slow drive-bys, and walking enthusiasts who stretched their necks as they passed her home, they would surely eat up every word she revealed in the paper. It mattered little to her if it came on page one or in a big full-color ad placed on the back. Maybe she would merit both.

And she'd do them all one better still: she would invite the whole town to her open house where they could ask all the questions they were asking each other, evaluate her genealogy, and figure out what the heck she was doing here.

Where others saw a mystery, Sam was ready to surprise them all with an open book containing her life story. More than anything else, she just wanted to come home.

In her darker moments, she knew why:

She had nowhere else to go.

EIGHT

Small Town

FOR DECADES, SAM LIVED near a big city where people came and went about their routines, and they didn't pay much close attention to each other. Being anonymous had its advantages, she must admit. But in a small town, that wasn't going to be possible. Not that she wanted to be unknown; just a happy medium between the two extremes.

"The open house is the Saturday after Independence Day, the height of the reservoir's tourism season," Sam told the weekly-paper's editor, Phil Sparks.

"Must be hard for you to imagine your sleepy little hometown so busy with the reservoir and all," Phil commented as he took her advertising information. At this weekly paper, the editor wrote ad copy as needed, as well as news articles and editorials. He was also custodian—and owner. "The reservoir is good for the town what with the new restaurants, a marina, and the art center. People who never gave Freedom a thought are now seeing it as something of a destination."

Sam explained to Phil how she decided to use locals to supply everything from eggs for breakfast to paint for the walls to remodelers for the bathrooms.

"I've hired painters from Uptown Hardware and contracted the more difficult household projects to Star-Spangled Remodeling," she told him. "It might be more expensive at times than the competitive city stores. I believe that the accountability is worth it. Smaller local businesses will appreciate the support and see that I'm investing in the community as well as in my own place. I'm hoping they'll feel a sense of ownership once they finish."

The editor agreed with her approach. "It's how communities used to work when people depended on each other for goods and services, and then still had to pass each other in the grocery store, and sit next to each other at the basketball game," Phil said. "It was personal then. It still is."

∽

SAM BRIGHTENED THE HOUSE with a new coat of white paint on the exterior clapboards, making the vintage hunter-green shutters pop after they got fresh, sudsy baths. The porch was newly furnished with a black all-weather wicker sofa, rocking chairs, and even a wicker porch swing, all ordered from Uptown Hardware. The cushions were a crisp red, yellow, and green stripe. A variety of floral-print pillows in coordinating fabrics were tossed on all of the seating areas. It was about comfort and beauty; creating a relaxing setting that her guests would enjoy.

Whenever she looked at the outdoor furniture, Sam longed for time to relax with magazines and a big glass of iced tea. How nice it would feel to be a bed-and-breakfast *guest* right about now in the setting she created. But if she took a break to sink into the plump cushions, the temptation would be to be done for the rest of the day, and she'd likely fall asleep as soon as she sat down.

There was just too much to accomplish before enjoying the fruits of her labor. Sam daydreamed about what life might be like a year or two from now when surely everything had smoothed into a calm routine, and she had a chance, at last, to relax on her own porch, in her own life. At least she had a plan for the future, and some days, what kept her going, working so hard, was the idea of looking back on her labor, and knowing that it was all worthwhile.

A unique feature of the wraparound porch was a large built-in gazebo entered through a set of double French doors in the dining room. In the gazebo area, Sam placed a round, black table and several chairs with cushions that matched the furnishings on the front porch. Already, she enjoyed her morning coffee and paper there, and she knew guests would find the area irresistible. From there, guests could walk to the front of the house and relax on the front-porch furniture, return back inside the house through the dining room, or take a walk around town.

These weeks of updating and decorating were giving Sam a chance to hear the house speak to her in the way that a house will do if you let it. The home showed her where to place furniture for how people really lived, traffic patterns, and where houseplants thrived in the best diffused light.

This house had seen many generations of Fosters, along with countless visitors. The rooms showed her how people liked to move about inside of them. If those walls could talk, the stories they would tell.

One change Sam made quickly was removing June Foster's blue-and-white French-print imported wallpaper from the kitchen and dining-room walls. The paper was lovely adornment, no question, and probably cost a mint to install at the hands of an interior designer, but Sam had to make the house hers, and this wallpaper was a personal taste of June Foster's.

In its place, the kitchen walls were painted the palest, buttery yellow, and the dining room a couple of shades closer to sunshine. The kitchen paint color was Roger's idea, in an odd way. It was the yellow that Sam saw him painting in the dream.

What floored her was her daughter-in-law's suggestion on the day Sam moved in. "You know," Sally told her, a thoughtful look on her face, "I'm seeing this kitchen in a sort of, I don't know, buttery yellow."

Yes, Sam had agreed. *That was the perfect color. Roger's color,* Sam thought.

The rooms were warm, inviting, and it felt like the sun enveloped the space, even on days when it wasn't shining. The light was strong here late into the day, and she would appreciate this fact for years to come on cold, dark winter days. Light was a good thing.

The windows were covered with crisp paper-white lace curtains, and while the rich, golden-oak hardwood floor remained in the dining room, the kitchen now sported striking black-and-white checked tile and new, white marble countertops ordered from a local stone carver who was well known regionally for his craft. The always-cool marble was quite a pleasant contrast to the warmth of the walls and wood.

Glistening crystal and antiques collected from Sam's and Roger's flea-marketing outings, and passed down in their families, added personality to the room. A freestanding Hoosier cabinet made in New Castle, Indiana, and spacious honey-oak built-in cupboards coordinated with the dining-room flooring and made handsome additions to the sun-dappled kitchen.

In the dining room, Sam's paternal grandmother's century-old white-and-gold dishes transformed a corner cabinet with sparkle. The long table sported seasonal dressings, but today, it wore an ecru hand-tatted heirloom that was handmade by Sam's maternal grandmother. It had lived with Sam in Green Hills for decades but was likely tatted right here in the county. Many of the furnishings had returned home, just like the new lady of the house.

Sam's bedroom suite was downstairs in the back of the house, behind the kitchen and laundry room, alongside a small, private den. It had been the personal living area of Mrs. Foster and was an ideal arrangement for a bed-and-breakfast in that the owner would have both privacy and easy accessibility to visitors. The four guest rooms were upstairs, each with a private bath. Getting those in order is what took so much of the spring and summer, as bathrooms had to be created from closets and some imaginative planning was involved.

Thank heavens for Monty Richards, owner of Star-Spangled Remodeling. He took a personal interest in seeing the project completed and showed up every day until it was both beautiful and meticulously done, never grumbling or perturbed no matter what considerable obstacle he found; just calmly working out the details to make things function just as Sam envisioned.

Monty had a vague memory of tagging along with his own dad out to the Jones homestead when he and Sam were kids and her family added an extra bedroom and bath. It was a connection that they both liked to try and remember, although details were scant. It made Sam seem, somehow, like a long-time neighbor to Monty, or at least not a stranger.

Gus approved of his mother's home improvements. "Mom, I'm really proud of you. You went after your and Dad's dream. It's really something here. Dad would be happy for you."

It was a nice compliment from a guy who generally preferred the new and trendy to the old and antique.

He encouraged his mother to make the open house as unpredictable as she had recently become to her own family and shake things up a little bit. "Your friend Mary Pat bakes those great sugar cookies; Gay has that granola that we all love, and then there's Cheryl's cheese dip. Your friends are awesome cooks, Mom. Let them lend you some hands that day. You know they'd love to help however they could. Just ask them."

Sam loved the idea. She would ask her friends to visit that weekend, unveil the place to them, and serve their signature foods at the reception. They were always asking what they could do to make the transition easier. This was a great way to take them up on their offers. "And guess what, Ma? Best of all I'll get home that weekend for the festivities."

It didn't escape either of them that he used the word "home."

"Mom, I don't care if you live on the moon," Gus said quietly. "Wherever you are is home."

Sam's friends agreed to her son's idea and even said that it would be fun; like a slumber party.

And not only would the event be about Sweetland, it would be about the town: a sort of best-of-Freedom-lifestyle display. Different areas of the home would be hosted by those whose talents Sam would showcase and recommend.

"Bev Grant will be in the kitchen and while explaining the décor will serve mini quiches made with eggs from her Yolks for Folks business," Sam explained to Gus. "Monty will walk around upstairs and tell everyone about how he coaxed a luxurious bathroom out of a coat closet and performed three other major bathroom miracles."

Sam loved the idea that the open house would celebrate everyone who was interested in making Sweetland a success.

The hostess would have no specific responsibility that day other than to visit with everyone who came by, and be available to roam from room to room as questions came up. Sam's stomach churned with excitement at the idea of so many former school pals and locals looking over her home. For that's what it had become. It was not just an economic opportunity. It wasn't even a Plan D, as she once called the idea of anything that didn't involve Roger. After all, this was still about Roger. It was his idea, really, and Sam never forgot that.

She planned to also share this magnificent space with friends she hadn't yet met, would nurture weary travelers and businesspeople that stopped by for a change of pace, or for a comfortable overnight stay. And she would welcome her own family and friends, and maybe someday, she hoped, grandchildren, when they came to see her.

She hadn't felt this positive about life since, well, since before Roger died.

Sam placed the full-page "Welcome to Sweetland" advertisement in the weekly newspaper. She giggled to herself at the thought of John Whetsel and Ellen Madison gasping. Neither of them had likely purchased ads in the hometown paper in quite a while, if ever.

One thing was for sure: the word was out. Most every person in United County knew that come three o'clock on Saturday afternoon, each and every one of them had a personal invitation to traipse through the doors of that stately, historic home, sample the best food that the region had to offer, and meet Sweetland: the county's newest business.

Sam was so wired on Friday night that she was sure she wouldn't sleep at all. She had been fluffing pillows, touching up baseboards, and shining every mirror and window in the substantial square footage of the place. It gleamed.

One more thing: Before she headed to bed there was something yet to be done. Her brother had installed the new sign out front earlier in the day. It felt like a ribbon-cutting moment; like the Freedom Business Buddies should give her a framed certificate. Yet no one was there, except for Sam, when right before bedtime, and without ceremony, she flipped a switch and the tasteful sign softly lit up the night, announcing to all on the street that a new business had arrived in an old home:

Sweetland of Liberty
Freedom's premiere bed-and-breakfast
S. Jarrett, proprietor

Sam crossed North Main Street and for a moment, stared back from the distance at her place with disbelief. There it was: her home, her business, her life. *Oh Roger*, she thought, *have I done the right thing? Is this where I should be?*

Then she went inside, took a hot, lavender-scented bath, and tucked herself into bed as the curtains fluttered softly in the windows and she heard the crickets around the small garden pond. Before she settled into a good night's sleep, she asked the Lord a question: *Will everything really be OK?* Then she thanked him for this provision, and for this beautiful home.

Yet, she still had some nagging doubts.

℮⁄ᴐ

AS SOON AS SAM'S friends from Green Hills were called about the open house, they got on the phone with each other to work out travel details. The women's lives were connected in various ways: attending church together, or their kids had been in the same school classes, or in the case of Mary Pat, they met through sharing the same baby-sitter when their children were small. The women truly were happy to have a way to help out their friend, and they looked forward to a fun weekend together.

Even so, the three women remained puzzled about Sam's move. She had never shared with them the dream about moving to Freedom that she and Roger had apparently hatched, and they each couldn't shake the feeling that Sam had acted on impulse. Sam's life was in Green Hills, and surely their friend was reacting to her losses, they agreed.

It was hard on all of them when Roger passed. Something in Sam, her usual spark, was missing after that. They had to admit that her energy seemed to have returned with this bed-and-breakfast operation. On the phone, anyway, she sounded like her former happy self.

"After Roger died, she never wanted to visit anymore," Cheryl told Gay. "If I met her for coffee, all she wanted to do was talk about him. I thought maybe she needed to turn her attention to other things, so I would change the subject when she brought up his name."

"I know what you mean," Gay said. "We asked her several times to join us for a night out, but she said she didn't want to be a third wheel. We didn't know what to tell her."

"I just hope that she did the right thing moving back to her hometown," Mary Pat offered. "I worry that her expectations may be way too grand. I just can't imagine her getting enough business to cover her expenses even. But I sure do wish her the best. And this weekend will be a lot of fun."

"We all can agree on that," Cheryl said. "I can't wait to see the house."

NINE

Welcome to Sweetland

BEFORE SAMANTHA'S EYES COULD even open on Saturday morning, she felt the butterflies, the ones that fluttered around her core, reminding her that this was it: the day she had long anticipated. Everyone would meet Sweetland. And the owner was now accepting reservations. Ready or not, the big day was here.

The feeling was familiar, but not common. She had felt this way prior to Ray and Sally's wedding. She was so incredibly excited then that she didn't get to bed until the wee morning hours after the rehearsal dinner and then woke up two hours later, unable to sleep. *It's my baby's wedding day!* she thought in that early hour, then decided that it really was too early to get up for good, or she would surely crash before the late-afternoon ceremony and look like a wilted flower before the wedding cake was even cut.

Yet somehow, Sam felt that more was expected of her today. As mother of the bridegroom, she knew her place wasn't as the hostess with the most-est. Her livelihood didn't ride on her actions during a magical wedding day. On that occasion, she could relax, to a degree, and just relish what was surely one of the happiest days of her life.

She hoped to experience that joy again one day when Gus found his bride.

The open house would showcase not only her new business, but the day was personal. It was oddly like throwing herself a welcome-home party, and yet, the guests, in many ways, were a mystery. She had no idea which people in the community would show up, or if, indeed, anyone would. It was like a home party selling kitchenware or costume jewelry and thinking how silly she would feel with all that pie and lemonade left over if no one came.

So the butterflies kept fluttering.

Sam poured her first cup of hazelnut-flavored coffee when her cell rang, and it was her older son's unmistakable ringtone. "Ray! This is it," Sam told her boy before he could even speak. She was wound tight.

"Yeah, Mom, Sally and I want to wish you the best today," he started, sounding none too happy. "But hey, we're not going to make it after all. I'm sorry, Mom. Sally is in the middle of a huge project here and—"

"It's OK, honey; don't sweat it," Sam said as though the news was happy. "I wouldn't have much of a chance to talk with you two today, anyway, and I'd rather save your time for when we can have a nice visit. You tell Sally good luck with the project."

She always cut that kid slack. But there was no way she would let it show to anyone how disappointed she really was. Besides, why should she expect her kids to drop everything and spend the day sitting around her porch? This was her job, not theirs. Not only was she a business owner and mom, she was a mother-in-law, and the last thing she wanted to do was be a nuisance to her daughter-in-law. Besides all of that, she was not about to be a spoiled brat like Joanna had been when Sam shared her plans. This was far too special of a day to spend even one single moment moping around—for any reason.

Sam was sure that Ray was still frustrated with her over this whole move. She'd have to win him over, and the best way to do that was to succeed, not be a problem, and to do it all herself, without assistance from either of her sons or daughter-in-law.

Gus would be there, and so would three of her closest friends from the Cleveland area. They would lend more than enough moral support to see her through. She would spend the day celebrating who was here, not pouting over who wasn't, and that included Roger. There was too much to do, anyway, to spend any kind of time in deep, dark thought.

Sam cleared her mind and sprang into action. She made her bed with extra care, showered, and slipped on the simple, apple-green, print sundress chosen for this very day. She was happy that it fit with a bit of room to spare. At least all of the summer's hard work had resulted in her dropping a few pounds. She tried to get her hair and makeup especially right and then added silver hoop earrings and looped a chain around her neck. It was a good thing that she got started dressing when she did because the doorbell rang early.

Jim and Jenny stood at the door, ready to help in whatever way Sam needed. She immediately put them to work setting up the beverage station on the gazebo as Sam flew around the house tweaking details. Soon after, a carload of her Green Hills friends—Cheryl, Gay, and Mary Pat—pulled up and offered hugs. They admired the house that took their friend away from them, and then they quickly got busy unpacking each of their prepared personal culinary specialties, along with more ingredients they needed to make items that had to be completed on the spot.

"It's just so good to see all of you! Let me give you the grand tour before things get really crazy," Sam said as they finished putting things away in the kitchen. They complimented Sam on the home, pointing out the antiques and other furnishings here and there that were so familiar from her place back in Green Hills.

"There's my Hoosier cabinet," Mary Pat quipped, dramatically stretching her arms across the front of it in as near a bear hug as one could give a large, chunky piece of vintage oak furniture. It was a standing joke between them that if Sam died first, Mary Pat got the cabinet. The friend had even made a deal with Gus that when his mother "goes," she would be coming right away for this piece of furniture.

Gus just laughed and shook his head. "No, I mean it," Mary Pat said. He was sure that she did.

"One day I can see you wheeling that thing through the nursing home," Sam told her friend, and they had a good laugh about the mental picture it created. Gosh, she missed these women. She felt a stab of homesickness for Green Hills; for her old life; for Roger.

Sam shared a good many years with them on the ball-field bleachers, and during community gatherings and girlfriend lunches. They'd logged hours of phone conversations.

They'd also traveled together on occasion when one or the other of them needed a trip companion. But five hundred miles and change didn't make for an easy excursion for women with full-time jobs, busy households to manage, and family commitments of their own. It was far enough that they, sadly, wouldn't be able to stay in Sam's life in any kind of routine, face-time way. Sam knew this and reasoned that if she could see them even once a year from now on, well, that would be a treat. They would have to work at maintaining their friendships. But they would do whatever it took, with or without physically being together.

Sam had taken all of them by surprise with her purchase of the old house, and none of them had yet seen the place. This was, in fact, the ladies' first trip to Freedom. Sam didn't want them to visit until everything was just right. She knew them well and didn't want to hear them second-guess her intent or raise questions about her sanity over this undertaking. She had enough of those thoughts without theirs. She wanted them to see Sweetland at its best. And she wanted to be at *her* best too.

"And there are your Grandma Jones's dishes," Cheryl pointed out, as they were arranged just so inside an oak china cabinet that Roger and Sam inherited from his folks.

"I've always loved how you blended both of your family's heirlooms, and I see that the move here hasn't changed that," Gay said. The antiques were always a comfort to both Sam and Roger; reminders of loved ones who had gone on.

"If anything, girls, my commitment to heritage is even stronger now; but be sure, not just my family's, or the Fosters' heritage. I want this place to be so welcoming and encouraging to strangers that when they come here, it's like being with the ideal version of extended family; like seeing the proverbial great-aunt who couldn't wait for their arrivals, and who has the bed made up just so in their honor, and who even has some goodies in the oven just for them. I'd love for them to consider Sweetland their home away from home."

Cheryl said, "Everything is just beautiful, my friend. I can see your vision for this place. I miss you to death, but this house—it's amazing."

And so it was. The dining room sparkled with polished silver that had belonged to Roger's grandmother. The table glistened from the lemon polish, and each curtain, table linen, pillow, and floral arrangement was in place.

Jim and Jenny finished their assignment filling trays with Mary Pat's sugar cookies, and slipped onto the front porch to be out of the way from the hubbub while Sam visited with her friends in the kitchen. Before long, Sam heard voices and laughter outside, and when she glanced out, she was pleased to see that Gus was seated on the porch, talking with his aunt and uncle. She showed the ladies to their rooms and gave them time to freshen up after their drive while she went to greet Gus.

"Ma! Hey, I'm here."

"So you are, kiddo. I'm so glad you could make it."

"Wouldn't miss it," Gus said, hugging his mother.

Sue Conner walked across the lawn to see if there was anything she could do to help. She greeted Jim and Jenny and sat down with them for a visit. Sue was proving to be a friendly and welcoming neighbor, and one who would be a joy to live next to in the years ahead. In fact, she seemed genuinely excited to have the inn next door. It wasn't just a matter of being nosy. This could become a true friendship.

Monty arrived before the crowd and caught Sam off guard. She had never seen the fellow without his tattered painter pants and tool belt, but today, he was sporting dress khakis and a crisp button-down shirt. He seemed relaxed hanging out on the front porch with the Joneses.

He wasn't keen on marketing his work in a big way, and didn't need to, either. Everyone in town knew what he did and where to reach him if they needed his services. He'd never even had a calling card as his business dated back to his own grandfather. He was the third generation to work in the remodeling business, and had been at it since he was a little kid, tagging along with his grandpa and dad.

But if Mrs. Jarrett wanted him here, he was happy to oblige. He was grateful to get the chance to work on a showplace like the fine old Foster home, and he liked the energy and vision that Sam brought to town. Yes, he thought having a bed-and-breakfast in Freedom would be a great addition to the town. There was no place else like this for people to stay. This home would fill a need in a tasteful, friendly way.

Lisa Brown from Lisa's Landscapes was situated by the garden fish pond, anxious to talk to anyone who wanted to chat about the work her team (meaning she and her son, Jake) had done on the property, including the stocked fish pond out back. Holly Smith of The Queen's Table was stationed on the gazebo where she would serve beverages and discuss her tea-and-dessert catering service.

Sam took a moment and walked deep into her back lawn looking back at the house and the property and feeling so grateful for all that was before her. All of these people! They had shown up to support her. She was so blessed and grateful. She wanted to inhale the moment, savor it, and put it in a bottle to keep. But she had to get busy.

The stage was set.

TEN

Open House

ALTHOUGH THE OPEN HOUSE wasn't scheduled to start until three, as was plainly stated in Sam's full-page *Times* ad and on the personal invites she mailed to friends and family members, the point mattered little to the fine folks of United County. Good thing that the food and the help all arrived early, because by two thirty, something of a crowd had assembled on the lawn and on the front porch.

Sue, who visited with Jenny for a good hour that morning, was back bearing a gift. This time it was a homemade pie made with handpicked cherries.

"You, your Ohio friends, and your boy can enjoy this tonight when things slow down and everyone else has left," she said. "And welcome back to Freedom. I sure do hope you make a go of it. If you and your people ever need an extra place or two to park, well, I don't have so much company, and they sure are welcome to use my driveway."

Sam was touched by the gracious generosity of her new neighbor and friend.

Others streamed in and looked her over good and proper, trying to form quick opinions about this woman who was standing in June Foster's house. Some guests didn't even care so much about Sam but had waited their whole lives to see inside this landmark residence.

She could have sold tickets.

Then the occasional school chum came through as Sam tried to put the name with the face, and then like camera lenses adjusting just so, with the subject gradually coming into clear focus, Sam laughed with delight that she suddenly recognized the person. They visited for a moment until the next guest showed up and the process started again. Sam was amazed by how many folks from her past came through the door.

The Reverend Stan Bennett from Freedom Community Church paid his respects and asked Sam how she liked the sound on Sunday mornings of those newly refurbished church bells.

"They are great, pastor. They have such a clear, sweet quality. It's the first time in my life I've heard church bells on a Sunday morning from my own home. We couldn't hear them out in the boonies when I was growing up. And our home in Green Hills was too far in the suburbs. The sound is a joy every Sunday."

"They are on remote control now. We push a button and off they go," the minister said. "Would love to have you join us on Sundays, Mrs. Jarrett, and please, call me Stan."

"Stan, I might do just that. I haven't settled on a church yet. But finding one is a priority on my to-do list. I sure do appreciate the invitation. Oh, and please, I'm Sam."

Her insurance man, Kurt Cordell, got there early, which was unfortunate, as he didn't much appreciate seeing the most-senior ladies in the crowd climbing the steep flight of stairs. Possible claims if they fell, you know. He frowned to himself as he considered the consequences if one of them slipped off of her high heels. He was thinking through another angle too. Not only was he worried for his policyholders, he was a volunteer EMT and didn't want a call to haul them out of there.

Being in his line of work for so long made him think twice about things that never occurred to the general public, he thought. He bore his burdens silently, but his face wore a serious expression at all times as though disaster lingered just around the next corner, because he was convinced that it did.

Apparently an open house was the equivalent of an early-bird special to the town's residents who showed themselves today in great numbers. By midafternoon, that starting round of guests, along with the entire membership of the Freedom Literary Club, had moved through the house and wouldn't need dinner that night, either, from their considerable grazing, as well as the fact that for many of them, supper hour had arrived.

By late afternoon, the front porch was bursting with Sam's extended-family members. She was delighted when several Joneses appeared in a wave of support. They hung out with Jim and Jenny on the porch before trickling through the house. "I can't believe it," Sam exclaimed. "This is like a family reunion. Thank you all so much for coming out today. I appreciate it so much."

Mary Pat came through with a tray of floral-shaped sugar cookies and offered them to the Jones family members. "We've got to get a group photo of everyone!" she insisted after meeting the relatives whose names she had heard her friend mention through the years. It was fun for the friend to put those names with faces at long last. Mary Pat had always known how much Sam had missed, and longed for, that close contact with extended family, the kind that Mary Pat had with her own loved ones in Green Hills, which was the hometown she never left.

"Aunt Sam, we'll all be back tomorrow for Sunday dinner," joked niece Lindsay, and everyone laughed.

Sam turned around and found standing there her high-school friend, Angie. They caught up on life and then, a surprise. "Sam, I am actually here on business. My daughter is engaged to be married next year and her future in-laws are coming in two weeks for a weekend visit to meet our family. Could we possibly book their stay here?"

This was the moment Sam had hoped would happen today.

"Absolutely, Angie. And do you know what else?" Sam inquired. "This makes my first paid reservation. Thank you."

But it wasn't the only one. Mary S. Williams of the Freedom Literary Club phoned Samantha a little bit later in the evening. Apparently the entire membership was so delighted with the bed-and-breakfast that the ladies took a special vote via the emergency telephone chain and decided to book the parlor and Sam's homemade refreshments for afternoons on the last Thursday of each month, on a trial basis, of course, to make sure that they liked it.

They were tired of thirty years' worth of rotating meetings in one another's living rooms. It was time for a permanent site, they decided, almost in unison. Sam had special day rates for clubs and for individuals who wanted to use her place for social events such as bridal and baby showers. The literary ladies had money in the treasury, and Sam was more than happy to host them. It was a win-win arrangement for everyone involved.

And there was even more good news. Another long-ago friend, Pam Clevenger, recently returned to Freedom after decades of living in Atlanta. She, too, was a widow, but wouldn't be for much longer. Using social media, she had rediscovered an old high-school flame, and they were now planning a small October wedding in their hometown. They had not settled on a place for the ceremony and reception. That is, they hadn't until Pam saw the ad for Sweetland of Liberty. "I just knew this house would be perfect for our wedding," she told Sam. "Do you suppose I can book it for both the wedding and reception? It will be a small gathering."

Sam was delighted. "A wedding at Sweetland! This is so exciting, Pam. Let's do it."

Samantha bounced from one room to the next, explaining everything again, and again from how many years the house had been in the Foster family, to how she thought to transform it into a small inn. The answers were at once simple and complex. There were long versions, and short ones too, depending on how much people wanted to hear. It had been a retirement idea that she and Roger had just begun to discuss before he passed away. That was one truth. But there were others. Her career had ended. She was alone, and where do you want to turn when you are scared and alone?

She wanted to go home.

The background was filled with a rich blend of light, muffled chatter from locals who were touring the guest rooms. Jenny decided to check the refreshment trays and ice buckets in the second-floor library. As she arranged more cookies, she overheard the librarian, Amy Howard, in the midst of an intense conversation with her mother.

"All I know is that I was getting dressed to come here when I heard her car come roaring into his driveway," Amy said. "I looked out the window to see what the commotion was about, and I saw that he was looking out the door, and she was screaming at him. She said, 'How could you let June Foster sell my house? My house! This is not over. Not by a long shot.'"

Jenny heard no names mentioned in the exchange, but she had a pretty good idea who the lady was that Amy was referring. She and Jim didn't meddle in the doings of their family members and had always preferred keeping silent on situations that didn't directly concern them. But they had been hearing some mutterings from people in town about Jim's sister's return.

Some folks had been complaining that there was no need for an inn; that it was an awfully brazen thing for Sam to do, just march into town, open such a place, and then announce it in the paper in a full-page advertisement—color even. Who did that? Certainly no one they knew.

Jim and Jenny kept quiet. Samantha was back, and they were glad about that. But understand it? They couldn't truly say that they did.

By the time the event ended, Jim and Jenny asked if they could do anything else to be helpful. They had been such a godsend, greeting guests on the front porch, helping with the food, visiting with people, and before that, Jim installing the sign. Jenny kept to herself the content of the conversation she overheard.

Finally, with everyone except her close friends and Gus gone, Sam plopped down on the sofa and smiled widely. "Well, we did it! We introduced Sweetland to society. Do you realize that I have three actual bookings already?"

"That's great," said Gay. "It really is. I can't get over how many people filed through here today."

Sam saw something troublesome in her friend's face. Their eyes met.

"I don't want to spoil a great day, and it was a great one, Sam, but I overheard some talk from your insurance man and some other guy in a suit. I think his name was John."

"That was probably John Whetsel. He's a lawyer in town. In fact, he's June's attorney, and the one who put together the paper work for purchase of the house."

"Well, I guess I don't really know, only that apparently, you were not the only one who had her eye on this home." She told Sam about a conversation referring to an Ellen somebody.

"It seems that this Ellen, for what it is worth, which may be nothing, remains very angry that she didn't get to buy your house. That's what the two men kept talking about."

Sam tried to remain lighthearted. "I can't say as I blame her about wanting to live here, obviously, but the point is: she *didn't* buy it; I did. Sweetland belongs to me. Ellen will simply have to adjust, and find herself another house. Surely it won't be too difficult to do that. There are a lot of beautiful homes in the area."

With that, Sam quickly changed the subject.

The two visited a while longer until they noticed that the others weren't coming downstairs to join them, and there was no more chatter from upstairs. Apparently the other gals were ready to turn in. It had been a long day. They called down their good nights. The house was at last quiet.

"I need to hit the hay too," Gay told her friend. "So much for our rollicking slumber party. Seriously, thanks so much for making us a part of the big day. We won't forget it any time soon."

"I really don't know how I would have done it without you, and the other girls," Sam responded. "Your food was spectacular but your company was priceless. It meant so much to have you all here."

With that, they both went to bed.

Sam didn't want to let on how troubled she was by what Gay had overheard.

ᘓ

RAY JARRETT WAS FEELING more than a tad guilty. Maybe he should have made the effort to attend his mother's open house, after all.

"I just don't understand her thinking these days," he told Sally. "If this is some kind of ploy to get us all to go and spend countless vacation days refinishing antique furniture, or creating fish ponds, she has got to figure out quickly that those things are not going to happen."

Ray sounded adamant. But nevertheless, it bothered him that she hadn't called to update him on all of the day's festivities. He'd had to text Gus and get the lowdown. Maybe he would phone his mom tomorrow. At least Gus had been there to represent all of them.

Their mother was going to have to figure things out on her own, and if she couldn't, she'd have to sell out and go back to Green Hills. She should have stayed there in the first place, Ray felt.

∽

GUS HIT THE SEND button on the cell phone, replying to his brother's text message. The day had gone well for their mother, he was happy to report. He didn't see why his older bro was so worried about her. People were always getting all stressed out about other people's business.

The boys remembered when they were small how exciting it was every time they packed up and headed to Indiana to visit the grandparents. There were a few memories of playing out on the farm. Once they had an Easter-egg hunt with the cousins, but as soon as Ray, then Gus, got busy with sports and school activities, their trips were fewer. Then it seemed that their mother went to Freedom alone a lot because her folks had taken ill at about the same time and she spent a good many weekends visiting on her own. As little kids, they didn't think that much about it. That was just how it was.

After the loss of their dad, Ray kept pointing out that the day would come when their own mother would need more care. Ray seemed to dwell on that point, and actually, he and Gus had words about it.

"Bro, Mom is fifty. Let's not put her in layaway in the old folks' home just yet," Gus told Ray.

"You may be too young to remember, Gus, but I do. I recall all those trips Mom made when Grandpa Jones got sick, and then how she had to deal with Grandma's illness and then later, when the family sold the Jones farm. I just don't want to have to deal with all of that stuff. Not that anyone does, but I guess her moving there brings back those memories, and they aren't good ones, either."

"Dude, you are getting ahead of yourself by decades," Gus said. "Besides, those things are all just part of life. We didn't expect Dad to check out so young but he did. You just never know what can happen and when or if it does, you deal with it. Don't go all morbid on me."

Ray was more conservative than his brother in his thinking and the way he led his life. Gus thought life was made to take chances, and the one their mom was taking made sense to him. What also surprised him was how much fun he was having this weekend. It was good to see the extended family; meet some of Mom's old friends and begin to understand what the draw was to this place.

While Ray viewed visiting this town with dread, Gus didn't.

In fact, he looked forward to the next time he'd be back in Freedom.

ELEVEN

Sunday on the Porch

SAM AWAKENED TO THE Freedom Community Church bells chiming beautifully, and she thought of Stan, smiling as he hit the remote-control button. Even though it was mid-July, the old house's rooms remained cool, thanks to the enormous trees careening into the sky all around the lawn, the thick walls, and cross-ventilation. Still, it wasn't like her to sleep in. She vowed that next week, if she didn't have guests, she'd be in a pew. She'd check out Stan's church.

Sam was grateful and prayed:

Lord, thank you so much for this beautiful home; for this new start in life. Thank you for the great turnout yesterday; for my wonderful friends visiting right now. Amen.

Sam's friends had instructed her to sleep as long as she possibly could, and then they'd switch roles and play innkeepers themselves, preparing coffee and breakfast, and they'd all dine together with Gus on the porch before they went their separate ways.

Much as she hated to see them all leave, and was so grateful that they were here, she had to admit that she needed a day to completely rest. The Lord knew what he was doing when he gave people Sundays off. The open house was a lot of work and stress. Sam could use a few weeks of vacation, but she would have to settle for the rest of today. She would do nothing.

She just didn't have it in her to rush. Not today. The open house had exhausted her. Not just the day itself, but all of it: the weeks of preparation, decorating, planning, meeting people, and getting everything in order for the big debut. It wasn't merely a want, but rather a need, to take the day off.

Sam thought about how a nap on the front-porch's wicker sofa was her one-and-only true goal for the day. But first, she enjoyed the pancakes, fruit, and coffee with her loved ones. She wouldn't even bother with makeup. If she had her way, after her friends and Gus left, she wouldn't see another soul, or speak another word, or even smile another smile. She was overdue for a block of solitude. And before noon, sure enough, her company was gone.

The phone rang, and it was Ray and Sally, piping in conference style, asking how yesterday went. "I'll have you all know, lady and gentleman, that I have three bookings, and one of those will be an ongoing, monthly, catered gathering as long as I do my job well, thank you."

The kids were upbeat, pleased, and even a bit surprised with the amount of business she inked in just one day. "Got to hand it to you, Mom," started Ray. "I figured they'd all come, eat up the pie, and leave. But three reservations; nicely done."

Sam laughed. "Young man, don't underestimate this old broad, even if I am your mother." She explained that there was plenty of food sampling going on around the inn, but she came out of the deal ahead because apparently Sweetland of Liberty was quite the place to be yesterday, and if the day was any indication, it was the town's new hot spot, to boot. "Well, as hot as a bed-and-breakfast in a small town could be," she told them.

After the pleasant conversation, Sam surveyed the downstairs, and everything was in order. Her friends had tidied up while she was still asleep, God love them. *Good enough for today*, she told herself, and slipped off to the porch where she planned to hunker down and read some of those magazines she subscribed to for the guests. She wasn't through the first article when the peaceful birdsong and the soft hum of cars passing by lulled her into a deep, soothing sleep.

"Samantha," she heard a voice whisper sometime later.

It took her a moment to realize where she was, and that someone was sitting directly across from her in a wicker chair, staring into her face. "Oh Samantha, dear; wake up."

Sam shot up on the furniture and out from her slumber to meet the gaze of a woman of about her own age, only thinner, certainly more smartly dressed, and in full makeup with stylish accessories. The lady was wearing a well-cut pink sundress, and her manicured nails were polished in the exact same shade. A string of good pearls surrounded her neck with matching earrings that peeked from under a perfect, chin-length, dark-brown page boy.

As the woman came more clearly into focus, Sam asked her how long she'd been sitting there.

"Oh, not long, Samantha. But apparently I'm quite late."

"Why, yes you are if you mean for the open house. It was yester—" Sam explained.

"Yesterday," Ellen interrupted flatly. "Yes, I saw the advertisement in the paper. And quite an ad it was too."

Suddenly, things became clear.

"Oh my goodness," Sam said, her voice rising. "Ellen. Ellen Madison. I'm sorry, hi. It's been, shall we say, a few years, since high school. You look great."

Ellen did not return the compliment. Sam registered that and was suddenly self-conscious about her own appearance. She just hoped that she hadn't been drooling in her sleep. Her face colorless, she was wearing cut-off sweatpants and an old Green Hills High School baseball T-shirt she threw on when she cleaned.

She didn't look like she could manage anything in that outfit; certainly not a new business. Her hair was a mess, she could feel, as she ran a hand through it. She should never have come out here on the front porch of her home, her *business*, looking like this, even if it was a Sunday afternoon, and she wasn't expecting anyone. It was far too public of a setting to be found *sleeping*, of all things.

"I must say, Samantha Jones, you really took me by surprise," Ellen offered, leaning forward as though about to ask something highly personal. She lowered her voice to a whisper, although there was no one else around to hear. "Come on now, you can level with an old pal. How did you find out, really, that June was ready to sell?"

Sam paused. Although she was generally open to a fault when speaking about herself and her motives, something stopped her from spilling all of her business. Ellen's tone made her feel, instinctively, like she had done something underhanded.

"Goodness, Ellen," Sam began with a nervous chuckle. "Isn't that a bit of a *personal* question? I mean, why do you ask? I was ready to make a change, and so was June. That's all."

"Well," Ellen said in the same low voice with which she had posed the question. "I am asking because I wanted to buy this house myself. In fact, I had been planning to do just that for quite some time. I had it on good authority that June was ready to list it. It just seems odd to me that all of a sudden, you enter the picture." She stopped there abruptly.

"Look Samantha," Ellen resumed, lifting both her voice and a crisp check from her small handbag. "I see you've gone to some additional expense here, and we both know this is a beautiful home with a sweet resale value. What will it take for you to sell this place to me here and now and be done with it at a tidy profit? It really doesn't matter to me who pockets the cash, you or June. And since June was, shall we say, less than cooperative with me, I am more than happy to do business with you. What will it be?"

"Oh, Ellen. No. Sweetland isn't for sale. It's not just a question of money. It's about a new life, about a dream of mine, and about returning home. It's about contributing something to this town."

Ellen didn't seem to register a word that Sam was saying. "But surely you have a *figure* in mind," she continued. She believed to her core that everyone and everything had a price. "I mean, look at you. You are obviously exhausted. Do you really think you can *keep up* with all of this?"

"Actually, no, Ellen. The truth is that I do not have a figure in mind. Some things are more precious than your blank check there," Sam said, trying with increasing effort to sound light. She hoped her voice wasn't cracking. "In answer to your question: Yes. Yes I do, indeed, think that I can *keep up*, as you put it."

With that, Ellen returned the check to her purse and snapped the latch shut. Her dark eyes flashed with an intensity that startled Sam. The visitor's entire demeanor had snapped, along with the latch.

"All right then, Samantha," Ellen said, her voice back to conversational volume. "We will just see about that. I thought we could do this nicely, like the ladies we are. But I see that you don't play nicely, do you, Samantha? Sweetland of Liberty, you call it? Really, now, how very quaint. How *corny*.

"Do you want to know a secret?" Ellen asked and then whispered the answer to her own question. "I never did care for you."

Sam felt the hair rise on the back of her neck; a reaction to the startling insult. She couldn't believe the unpleasant words that she was hearing on an otherwise pleasant Sunday afternoon. She didn't understand what was happening on her own front porch in her own hometown. She could not speak. Ellen's voice filled the void.

"Samantha Jones, oh, excuse me, *Jarrett*, is it? Well, write this in your guest book: I will have this house, my friend. You don't know what you've gotten yourself into. No one—and I stress to you *no one*—messes with me. You will regret the day you came back here, and you will regret this day too."

With that, Ellen stood up, straightened her well-fitted skirt, and smiling, walked off the porch and strode confidently down the street. Anyone watching from afar would have thought for sure they had just viewed two old friends having a nice chat on a front porch.

Those looking on would have surely thought that the scene before them resembled something out of a painting. One that depicted the charm and grace found in a small town. A town like Freedom, Indiana.

TWELVE

The Second-Guessing Game

FOR THE LONGEST TIME, Sam sat frozen on the front porch. Had she dreamed what just happened? And what, precisely, *did* just happen, anyway? She was offered a blank check to sell away Sweetland, and she declined to take it. She was—was she not?—*threatened*? Ellen told her she would regret this day. What did that even mean? What made Ellen Madison think that she had any right to threaten anyone about anything? Why did this house mean so much to the woman that she couldn't simply find another one and move on with her life?

As evening fell, Sam tried to clear her head by turning her attention to the week ahead and double-checking the scribbles in her planner. She would start the week busily because early Monday she expected some tourism bloggers who wrote about bed-and-breakfasts. They were coming on the heels of a Midwest travel-writers' conference. She couldn't cancel, and why would she, anyway? Ellen was not going to change her life or her plans.

On Tuesday, *The Daily Banner-Gazette* would be here for a Sunday homes-section spread. The reporter pitched it to Sam like she was selling the idea.

"*The B-G* is the area's largest newspaper and has nice circulations in a couple of regional college towns," the reporter said. "Parents of college students would make a fantastic client base for you."

Then Wednesday, Sam was speaking to the United County Library Board about her new business.

There was a lot to do, and she wasn't wasting a minute. The reporter seemed to lift the words out of Sam's mind. "The time to get the word out about your place is now while it is still something new and different; something to talk and read about."

Sam felt she needed to accept every offer that came her way. The opportunities might not present themselves again. People might soon tire of this old house.

She made herself a cup of decaffeinated green tea and decided to turn in at ten. She had plenty more things to get done as there were never enough hours. The bills were stacking, there were thank-you notes to write about the open house, and much more to see to as well.

Someone years younger could work until the wee hours, be up again at six, and not think a thing about it. Sam used to work like that too when she was younger. Come to think of it, she had two active children around the house in those days, a husband, a household to run, meals to get on the table, a full-time job, and often ill parents who were more than five hundred miles away.

How had she gotten it all done back then? She had no idea. But she *had* gotten it all done, and she would get done what was on her plate now, as well. She had to make this work.

As she walked through the house, switching off lights and bolting doors, Sam thought about how people didn't usually lock their doors in small Hoosier towns. It was one of those best-kept secrets that really wasn't a secret at all to the locals but would surprise city people to no end if they realized that fact. Yet tonight, Sam felt the need for an extra measure of security after the startling porch encounter earlier in the day. She was rattled.

Sam thought about giving one of her Ohio friends a call and filling her in on what had happened on the porch. But by now, all of them would be settling in after the long drive back to northern Ohio from Freedom, and they surely would not appreciate a sad story at this hour. They had work tomorrow. Sam felt selfish for even entertaining the idea.

There was no way she would trouble the boys with all of this, especially now, on a Sunday night. Ray called that morning and was confident, surprised even, that she was doing so well. She would not dispel that notion just a few hours later. She'd seen Gus off earlier, and everything for her seemed to be going not just good, but great. No, this was *her* problem. She had to show her loved ones that she could handle things—even bad things.

Maybe this storm would pass before anyone else even had to know.

She never missed Roger more than at this moment. In a marriage, this was when they could at last settle in and talk about the day, the future, and the past. They could bundle up all the loose ends of the week and declare that tomorrow would be better, that there was nothing that the two of them, with God's help, couldn't overcome. And then, they would go to sleep, nestled close, confident in an ability to handle whatever came their way. It still startled Sam that she no longer had a marriage partner to lean on.

What had she done in coming back to Freedom? It had been more than two years of grief, adjustments, fears, hard work, then hope, and tonight, disappointment. She returned home for peace and a new start, and now both of those things were being challenged mightily. In fact, she felt that she was up against a struggle more powerful than she even had words to describe. A wave of panic swept through her. She tried praying, but second-guessed her words, even with the good Lord.

The boys had been so proud of how their mom had gotten through the funeral, the months after, and how strong she had been. Only she hadn't been strong. She had been devastated, and scared to death.

She was still scared to death.

୧୬

"HERE'S YOUR COFFEE, SAM," Roger would tell her every morning as he brought it to her while she was still in bed. It was her cue to sit up and comment on the morning TV news while he got dressed. They didn't talk much at that early hour, but there was a joint strength, a companionship, in just being together, having each other with whom to start, and then finish, the day.

Around lunchtime, the text would come from Roger. "What are we doing for dinner and what time?" he inquired, and she responded. If he got home first, he'd start something for them, or vice versa. They had long since given up sitting around the kitchen table in favor of feet up on the oak coffee table, the news on the tube again as the sun set.

It was a comfortable, companionable life. They loved each other. But now, he was gone. There was no discussion or anyone to share routine daily happenings with, let alone the big ones like uprooting and moving away and buying an expensive old house.

Sam started to drift off to sleep when, suddenly, she heard a pounding outside, possibly from the front door. For a moment, she froze in her bed. Then, she got up and grabbed Ray's old ball that bat she kept in the corner of her bedroom, behind the door, and gingerly approached the hallway.

Her mind raced. Who could it be at this hour? Was Ellen Madison back for another round on the porch? Was the house on fire—what?

She looked out the front door but didn't see anyone or anything. Then, she heard the pounding again, and when she got up the nerve to step out onto the porch, she quickly found her answer. The culprit was a downspout that had come loose and was beating against the house on this windy night.

The adrenaline surged through her body, and she knew going back to sleep would be impossible right now. So she switched on a light and went to the kitchen. She got a jump on the morning by preparing a breakfast casserole. When that was done, she cut up fresh fruit, placed it in her great-grandmother's crystal bowl, and slipped it into the fridge next to the casserole.

Once all of that was finished, she was even wider awake, so she assembled the fixings for her friend Gay's mother's classic, Good-As-Gold Granola, baked it, let it cool, mixed in the dried fruit, then measured out portions in several clear, plastic gift bags, and tied them up neatly with pretty ribbon bows. Those would go home with the bloggers as keepsakes promoting her inn. Nothing spreads the word like a little gift of remembrance.

By midnight, her mind and body were finally finished, and she crawled back into bed. She was too tired to even dream or feel annoyed by the downspout. The words from one of her favorite scriptures tumbled into her mind, from memory. It was Isaiah 65:24: "I will answer them before they even call to me. While they are still talking about their needs, I will go ahead and answer their prayers!"

She didn't know at this moment exactly what the Holy Spirit meant by that, but she had to believe that he was with her and that he understood her needs better than she did. And since she had no one else to comfort her now, she would try to relax and let him do the job.

Meanwhile, across town, Ellen Madison slept like a baby.

⁓

RAY WAS RESTLESS. HE was glad that his mother had enjoyed such a great weekend. He guessed that he was possibly wrong about her making a mistake. He felt bad that he hadn't even offered a better explanation about why they wouldn't attend the big open house. He knew the weekend had meant a lot to his mom, and he also knew that he was punishing her by not going.

His mother didn't talk about finances with him, but he figured that financially, this move must not be a stretch or she would have told him. Surely she wouldn't have done it if there had been anything truly risky about it. Would she? Between his father's pension, their parents' joint savings, and the sale of the home place, she had to be OK. Didn't she?

If there was any doubt about her ability to afford this thing, certainly his mother wouldn't just wake up one morning, drive off to Freedom, and buy a house. She seemed happy as a lark right now, and apparently, business was already thriving. The bottom line was that both he and Sally wanted to see his mother happy.

There was no use losing any sleep over this situation. Ray figured that his mother certainly wasn't.

THIRTEEN

Business as Unusual

SAMANTHA WAS CONFUSED.
Once she finally dropped into bed, she slept hard, and when the alarm sounded the next morning, it took a moment to remember that she was serving breakfast to guests. She had to get up, dressed and ready to showcase the place before she even remotely felt like getting the day started. It had been a short night. There would be no leisurely moments today reading the paper or watching the morning TV news shows while nestling her coffee mug.

There was also no time to dwell on yesterday's disturbing visit. In fact, in the light of a pretty new day, it seemed almost silly to feel intimidated by someone just because she was jealous over not getting to this house first. If Ellen wanted to be a bully, it didn't mean that Samantha had to respond.

༄

ELLEN ALWAYS BELIEVED THAT she was better than everyone else in Freedom, more entitled, somehow. As a kid, she wore the surname Madison on her sleeve, as though just because her ancestors settled in little old Freedom before most anyone else's, it gave her more importance in everything from cutting in the grade-school lunch line to playing lead in the high- school play and serving as cheerleader-squad captain. She was always in charge all right. She savored being the boss; the head of everything that interested her.

Ellen looked down on common farm girls like Sam. And now, she apparently thought the nicest house in town should be hers for the taking.

It was all childish, small-town malarkey.

Perhaps Sam romanticized moving back home to the point where she was blind to the negative aspects of living here. She had been so caught up in her own personal drama that it never even occurred to her that anyone would mind, let alone oppose, her return to town and opening this business. What could be more benign than a pretty B and B? Who could it possibly hurt?

What was that old saying?

Question: "What's the best thing about living in a small town?"

Answer: "Everyone knows you and your business."

Question: "What's the worst thing?"

Answer: "Same answer."

The refreshing thing about living somewhere other than where you grew up was that people evaluated you on *you* and your own actions and abilities, not on those of your family members, or who you went to the homecoming dance with sophomore year of high school. It just seemed crazy that Ellen was still at the same kinds of games she always played with people.

⁓

THE DOORBELL RANG AND Sam greeted the bloggers. She escorted them around the house. The table on the gazebo was set with her grandmother's good dishes, and Sam positioned the crystal bowl in the center of the table, next to the vase of multicolored flowers, freshly cut from the garden.

The trio first walked past the open staircase and into the kitchen where they saw the dining room and the French doors leading to the porch. The route was carefully planned to showcase that very view. It was perhaps Sam's favorite in the house, as it appeared straight from a home-décor magazine. This notion struck Sam the first time she was inside of the room, the day she visited June Foster and prepared a tea tray in the kitchen.

As if on signal, the guests let out relaxed sighs and then remarked how pretty things looked. Their reactions made Sam smile because everyone who came through had the same reaction. The writers took photos to go with their online pieces.

Sam knew that from the smartly updated kitchen with its clean, white-marble countertops to the stainless steel appliances and golden-oak cabinets, every attention was paid to detail, and that this house was well equipped to become a destination-overnight stay.

"I don't want to leave this kitchen," one blogger said, inhaling the scent of Sam's breakfast casserole that was warming in the oven.

"Well, I think you'll enjoy the gazebo on such a nice day," Sam said, motioning toward the doors and the porch.

With that, they went outside and sat down. Sam gathered and served the casserole and passed the fruit bowl. She filled their coffee cups and explained to them that she would just be enjoying coffee, but not eating, so that she could readily answer their questions in detail.

"This all looks so, well, effortless," one blogger began. "I imagine that you spend your days polishing silver and lounging on the front porch."

Sam nearly choked on her coffee.

"Don't I wish," she told the women. "I assure you there's a bit more to running a B and B than that. But yes, I have spent some time on the porch."

They asked about Roger and why Sam would leave her campus job. They wanted to know about her sons, and her local family too.

"I almost forgot," Sam said, wrapping up the interviews and photo sessions. "I have something for all three of you." With that she handed them the homemade granola, festooned with ribbon at the top. They were pleased, as she figured they would be. She'd be making plenty more batches of the cereal to keep on hand as a breakfast option.

"It's always nice to send visitors away with a little something special," Sam told the bloggers as they gathered their things. "Please consider coming back to Sweetland as guests," she told them." She planned to give such parting gifts to her paying guests too. Always end on a positive note, she knew from her years in public relations with the president.

The thought of the president and her old job gave Sam an unexpected stab. It still pained her to leave her career and the college in such an abrupt, negative way.

ᴄ━ᴏ

LATER IN THE DAY, she paid a visit to Sue Conner next door and returned the glass cherry-pie plate. Sam needed a little break.

It was such a nice evening, and it stayed light so late, that Sam drove out to the little country-church graveyard where many of her relatives were buried, including her parents, and grandparents.

Sam was not one to decorate graves for holidays, or even once a year for Christmas or Memorial Day, either. She knew that her parents were not really there, and honestly, she found the tattered remains of weathered fake flowers that some people left behind to be depressing. She would rather leave her parents' graves alone than have worn memorials lying around them like she sometimes saw on other stones.

But on this evening, she felt drawn to walk around the cemetery, and as much as anything remember the good people she recalled fondly from her youth, those whose names were now etched in granite. She strolled around, and reflected.

She thought about how her own mother had been a grave decorator, and every Memorial Day, Sam went with her to a couple of little remote cemeteries where they placed the flimsy plastic flowers on the tombstones.

In one small country cemetery, there was even a tiny dollhouse instead of a headstone, built as a replica of a real home, she supposed, on the grave of a little girl who died too young. For many years, inside the miniature abode were dolls who were forever taking tea, seated around a toy table laden with tiny china dishes.

It was bittersweet, fascinating to Sam, but the memorial was no longer there.

The parents of the girl had no doubt passed on long ago by now, and probably there was no one left, even, to keep up the small memorial house. Even a permanent graveyard structure had to have upkeep, and was certainly not immune from the elements.

Nothing in this world was permanent. Not a little girl who died before her time, and no doubt broke her parents' hearts; not the girl's parents; not her little replica house and tea set. Not even June Foster's house. One day, it too would be gone, and so would Sam.

But as she drove back toward town with the green of summer flourishing all around her, she hoped that God would give her some good years in this town before her time was over too.

Maybe the tiny dollhouse didn't succumb to the elements, Sam thought with a sudden fright.

Maybe the house was vandalized, ruined by people who didn't care who or what they destroyed; people who, in fact, enjoyed the act of destruction.

People who enjoyed destroying others.

FOURTEEN

Paper Work

THESE INTERVIEWS WERE GETTING old.

But even so, the time she spent with the newspaper was productive. Today, Sam served high tea at four o'clock, and the reporter said it was the most pleasant diversion she had experienced in her career writing about lovely houses for the Sunday paper.

The two, along with the paper's chief photographer, sat for a good long while and visited. The tea was in the front formal parlor. Sam was showcasing different aspects of the B and B for this article than the ones the bloggers were addressing. She served small cucumber sandwiches stacked on a tiered silver tray, freshly baked cranberry-walnut scones, and a strawberry-pretzel layered "salad" that was truly more dessert than salad. A variety of teas, served hot or iced, were offered with the reporter selecting a summer-peach blend.

"With any luck, larger media outlets will see my piece and get interested, generating even more attention for you, and readers for me," the reporter said. "Maybe it will even be picked up by the wire service."

Sam liked the sound of that. It was all part of building her platform to launch the business. She dispelled the notion many people have about B and B owners: the myth that their inns are hobby jobs, not serious businesses.

"In fact, most who own these places are more than serious about their work," Sam said. "It really is a business."

The reporter quoted her, and Sam hoped she hadn't sounded harsh. There simply was no perfect sound bite to convey such a thing in an article. The piece was about the joy of inn-keeping and Sam's return home. "I also have a catering business and would be happy to talk to any clubs about meetings here or with individuals about hosting showers or other social receptions."

The photographer recorded the kitchen, the gazebo, an outside overview, taken with the sign in the foreground, and interior shots of each of the four guest rooms upstairs, and the center library there where guests were invited to watch TV or relax with games and books.

Then they put together a video for the Internet package.

The writer had done her homework. She carried with her a thick, tattered file about the Foster family's roots in United County as described in many newspaper articles spanning many decades. All newspapers had morgues; permanent files where these clippings about people, places, and events were stored according to subject name for reference purposes. Nowadays, a newspaper morgue was no longer called that. Rather, it was an online archive, stored digitally.

"We are in the process of scanning all of the old clippings into digital files," the reporter said of the bulging envelope. "When I knew I was coming here, I went ahead and scanned in all of these, and once we do that, we are to dispose of the paper copies. I thought rather than toss out the file, you might enjoy keeping it."

Sam was impressed. "How thoughtful of you," she told the journalist. "I'll enjoy going through the envelope and learning more about this house and the Fosters. I truly appreciate your thoughtfulness."

She tucked the hefty envelope of yellowed clippings into the top drawer of the kitchen Hoosier cabinet.

Following tea, the journalists visited the flower gardens out back, and the outdoor photos were taken with Sam snipping blooms with the gazebo portion of the porch in the background. The reporter and photographer wrapped things up by late afternoon, and Sam sent them off with another of her specialties, small bags of homemade powdered laundry soap. There were recipes for it all over the Internet, and Sam had enjoyed making it herself for the Sweetland laundry as well as for sharing with guests.

"If you don't want to use it on your washables, leave the closed bag in your car. I discovered by accident that it makes a really aromatic car air freshener," she told them as they gathered their notebooks and photo equipment. "Even if you leave it in the car and never get around to using it as intended, surely you'll think of Sweetland."

∿

THE WEEK UNFOLDED WITH much on the agenda, and Sam was glad. She didn't want to flatter Ellen with giving her a moment of her thoughts. There was no reason to let a disgruntled competitor upset her.

Sam would just be glad when her life was more about changing sheets, serving breakfasts, and providing tourist information than it was about her own publicity tours.

Wednesday was the library-board presentation. The librarian, Amy, asked her to speak, and Sam thought: *Well, why not?* The board members appeared both attentive and receptive, and even better, no one dozed off.

"Sam, the board would like to know if you would consider serving as a member," Amy told her friend after the officials left. "They really liked what you had to say."

"Well, please tell them that I am honored and I will consider it, Amy," Sam responded.

Then Amy pulled Sam aside. "Before you leave, there's something else," the librarian confided. "I don't mean to be nosy, but Ellen Madison was in here yesterday asking me to make copies of some town regulations from the town-council and zoning-board binders we keep on the reference shelf. They had to do with businesses located on town residential properties, and about town ordinances."

"Oh, really? What does that have to do with me?" Sam asked.

"Well, it's just that, when I gave her the copies, she placed them in a file folder with the name Foster House on it. I only thought you should know," Amy responded.

Sam started to mentally process this information, but her cell rang, interrupting her thoughts.

"This is Patricia Edmond of Davenport, Iowa. Say, my husband Tim and I need to book a stay in September."

Excusing herself from the library to outside where the reception was clearer, Sam got out her planner and went over the details, telling Mrs. Edmond that the dates were perfect. She secured the credit-card information to hold the room. "What brings you to Freedom?" she asked.

"This is embarrassing, but we have to appear before your town court. It seems that my husband has been subpoenaed for having caught an improper fish."

Sam wanted to laugh, but Mrs. Edmond was serious. "We are not at all happy about having to travel back to your fair little burg over a dumb bass from the reservoir!" she said.

"Well, I do hope that your stay at Sweetland will be much more enjoyable than your town-court appearance, Mrs. Edmond. I will look forward to your visit. How did you hear about my inn, may I ask?"

Mrs. Edmond said when she called the town court, the clerk not only gave her the name of the B and B but the owner's name and phone number. *Well, well,* Sam thought. *Seems that the locals are spreading the word.*

Two more couples called on Thursday, and on Friday, a traveling businessman stopped by, hoping for an opening through the weekend as he had a meeting in a nearby city on Monday and needed quiet time to prepare his presentation.

Sam hadn't officially been open a week yet, but already she had an impressive number of bookings. Good thing she had several bags of the granola ready for their parting gifts.

The guests were kind and considerate of her time, and of the inn. One couple even made the bed in full before Sam could get to it to change the sheets. They left a note, "No need to wash our bedding. It's plenty clean enough. We'll return this evening after a day at the lake."

On Sunday, the newspaper article and photos filled a full page in the homes section. Sam was able to link it online to her own website, and before nightfall, three more reservations were made. Her website, created with some help from employees at the town's only computer shop, was getting hit hard, which was a good thing.

⁓

ON MONDAY OF THE last week of July, Sam had to plan for the Freedom Literary Club ladies who would be coming in for their first meeting Thursday.

Sam revisited her menu from the journalists' tea and created the delicate cucumber sandwiches, cut out with small cookie cutters in a variety of summer-themed shapes. This time she would have white-chocolate-dipped strawberries, and the dessert would be Sue's recipe for Mom's Spice Cake, along with the flavored-tea assortment.

She looked forward to Wednesday when she and Jenny would spend several hours together in the kitchen. Jenny enjoyed baking and had agreed to help Sam when she had catering gigs. Also, they planned to spend an afternoon together once a month to make the inn's signature sugar cookies from Mary Pat's recipe that Sam would keep on hand for guests.

"I've got an idea," Jenny offered. "How about if each month, the cookies have a theme to go with the season or special occasion? The cookies will be available around the clock in a big glass jar in the up-stairs library where you could also keep a mini fridge stocked with soft drinks."

Sam was delighted with both that idea and the opportunity to have her sister-in-law commit to spending quality time together every month making cookies.

She had another reason besides the paycheck to look forward to re-garding the Freedom Literary Club. The most-senior member was none other than June Foster, and she would be returning to her home for the meeting.

When Thursday arrived, the club's speaker, Jeanne Singleton, came early to set up some baskets and get organized as she was giving the program on her handiwork. Mrs. Singleton had been Sam's very own fifth-grade teacher, and she was a favorite, so Sam was delighted to have a few minutes to catch up with her in private. Moments like this were at the core of why Sam came home to live and work.

At the correct time, the rest of the ladies arrived. Last to enter the house was June Foster. They all gathered in the entrance hall and re-marked how beautiful the house was. It could have felt incredibly awk-ward to showcase updates and a redecorated home from the one Mrs. Foster had loved so well for so many years. But it was the mark of a truly gracious lady that Mrs. Foster put everyone at ease.

"Friends, hasn't Samantha done an exquisite job of transforming this old place?" The ladies lightly applauded. "I simply am in love with it and honored that others will enjoy it, delighted that I will indeed ex-perience it in an entirely new way as a guest."

During the new-business portion of the meeting, June Foster made a motion that Sweetland be the permanent home for the Freedom Literary Club.

"I second that," came a comment from behind the ladies. It was Ellen Madison standing in the doorway. Her presence startled them all. Apparently she had stepped in while the others were admiring the kitchen update.

"Well then," Mrs. Williams said. "All in favor say aye!" The motion carried unanimously. Except, and no one pointed this out, that Ellen did not respond, and was not even a member of the club. They would all have plenty to say about that later, privately, to each other as they shared their "concerned news."

Following Mrs. Singleton's program, Sam passed plates of savories and sweets and kept the hot tea flowing from her collection of pretty teapots.

As she heated the final kettle's content of water, she turned around to find Ellen staring at her—again. The others were chatting in the parlor. "Well, well, Samantha," she said. "Nice little place you have here. Too bad you can't keep it."

"Just what do you mean by that, Ellen?" Sam asked.

"You'll see soon enough," Ellen replied. "Very soon, in fact."

With that cryptic message, she turned and left the house.

This was the second time that Ellen rendered Sam speechless and feeling like a whipped puppy, uncertain of what to do, say, or how to act after feeling like grenades were launched into the pit of her stomach.

"More tea, anyone?" Sam asked as she entered the room again. She hoped that they didn't notice that her hands were shaky. She forced herself to act normal.

"Oh, heavens no," they all seemed to say in unison as though in rehearsed rounds of a song. "It was delightful, just wonderful," said Mrs. Hamilton. With that the ladies got up and were on their way.

"As treasurer of the club, it falls on me to settle up with you, Samantha." Mrs. Hamilton wrote a single check for the amount due, to the even penny.

Sam had a permanent monthly booking. And unlike the more anonymous life in the city, the loyalty factor was tremendous in a small town. If Freedom society women booked you permanently, you could about guarantee that a quarter century from now, if it's the last Thursday of the month, you had yourself the ladies of the Freedom Literary Club seated in your front parlor.

༄

THE NEXT DAY, SAM received certified mail from the Freedom Zoning Board.

The formal letter stated that the posted, electronically lit sign on the property located at said address was in violation of a specific town law and that said sign must be removed within ten days of receipt of the letter to avoid further action.

The next page read something even more unsettling.

It said that the zoning board had neither received nor approved any request for approval to operate a business on residential property, and therefore, no business could be legally conducted at the site, effective immediately.

Sam was breaking the law. Two laws.

She had to sit down.

Then she called Jim.

FIFTEEN

Call to Arms

"WE HAVE TO TALK," Sam said seriously when her brother answered the phone. "Something terrible has happened, Jim."

"Are you all right? The boys? Sally?"

"Yes, we are all fine; it's not that," Sam said. "But Jim, I may lose this house."

"Should we come right over?"

"Could you, please?"

"We'll be there shortly."

Sam started pacing around the kitchen, then sat down at the dining-room table and spread out the official documents in front of her. She was confused. How could it be that she was doing something wrong? Who was she hurting? All she wanted to do was run a simple little business, and meet a need in a somewhat creative way, never done before in this town. What was the big deal? The last thing she ever had in mind was stirring up any kind of conflict.

When, if ever, would her life smooth out from one unexpected trauma after another? When could she start recovering the money that this house was devouring?

When Jim and Jenny got there half an hour later, Sam motioned for them to come on in and back to the dining room. They sat down opposite from her at the table, and she scooted the papers around facing their direction.

Her brother and sister-in-law looked concerned, not knowing what to expect, but sensing from Sam's demeanor that this was serious business.

"Here, read this," Sam said, the words catching in her throat as they tumbled out.

"Well, this is a problem," Jim said after a couple of minutes. "I'm guessing, then, that you didn't file any zoning-variance requests before opening the place."

"You're guessing right, Jim. I bought the house, filed the typical real-estate papers that Dan Frame and John Whetsel put before me, but a zoning variance? Well, no. It never even occurred to me. And no one, certainly not the real-estate man or the attorney, or even the people at the mortgage company, mentioned anything of the kind, either. This is the first I've heard of it. And what a grand way it is to announce it to me too—certified mail."

Sam slumped back in her chair, deflated, as her brother and Jenny methodically read every line in the new documents.

"Well, it appears that you filed everything you should have for a residential property," Jim said. "But the bad news is that because it is also a business, the paper work is not complete. You would never have bought it if your plan was to simply live here only, with no business involved. From the beginning, you had every intention of acting as caretaker of your business, and earning a profit."

"That's right, yes, of course. Oh, Jim, I didn't realize I had to do anything else. What a fool I am!" Panic was setting in as Sam tried to think what this would mean to her future.

Jim hated to see his sister so distraught. "Don't get all worked up just yet. It's probably a technicality with an easy remedy. Don't get upset until you know more."

Why did it not occur to her that there would be special paper work to file, and gain approval of, before she could open her business? *Maybe because I've had about a million other things on my mind besides, that's why,* Sam thought.

"I knew I had to have the United County Health Department clear the kitchen and provide a permit so I could prepare food for guests,"

Sam told them. "Look, it's in that wooden frame hanging there next to the fridge," she said. "The inspector came out, and it was no big deal at all. But until now, no one let on that anything else was missing. What a grand 'welcome home' this is!"

"It could be," Jenny pointed out, "that no one in this community, or in authority either, would have ever said anything about it unless there was a complaint. Do you have any idea about who might have objected to your business being in town?"

Sam suddenly felt the blood rush out of her face. "As a matter of fact, I do," she said, remembering Ellen's words on the porch, then those in her own kitchen during the literary-club meeting. And there was the library incident when she wanted those copies of town ordinances made.

So this is how it was going down, after all. Ellen told Sam that she would regret the day she bought the house from June Foster, and regret that horrible incident on the porch when she refused to sell out. It was all beginning to make a warped kind of sense. Ellen would try to force Sam's hand, and just maybe Sam would have no recourse but to give up on her dream. Or she would get scared over some legal papers and run for the hills—back to Green Hills, in fact.

Sam had hoped that she wouldn't have to tell anyone about the day on the porch, or about the literary club meeting when she had been briefly, but dramatically, confronted by Ellen. She didn't want to share the burden with her family. Surely she could deal with it alone. Besides that, it was all so embarrassing.

But now it seemed ridiculous to think that she could handle this without both divine intervention and the help of people who were in her camp. It was time to come clean about what, and whom, she was up against. Sam shared with Jim and Jenny the details about what happened with Ellen on the porch and then again right here in the kitchen during the club meeting and how she seemed out for no good.

"Ellen admitted that my purchase thwarted her plans to have this place for herself. She couldn't understand my timing."

"Wow, Sam. Why didn't you say anything to us about all of this? You didn't have to deal with this all alone," Jim said. "Do your boys know what you've been through with that woman?"

She told them that no one knew until now. She didn't want to appear unnecessarily paranoid or bother other people with her problems when nothing would probably ever come of Ellen's bullying, anyway. She wanted them to see that she could handle her new life.

"I haven't admitted this to you, or to anyone else, for that matter. But Ray was really angry about my move here," Sam offered.

"On top of that, my boss said it was foolish from the beginning. My financial advisor back in Green Hills thought I'd lost my mind when I dug so deeply into our investments," Sam told them, choking back tears. "I left all of my friends behind and forced myself, front and center, right here on North Main Street, into all of your lives. I didn't feel I was in any kind of position—and still am not—where I could dump my issues on anyone else. All of this is my own doing, no one else's, so I figured it's my problem to work out."

Everyone was silent for a minute as Sam's words sunk in and the gravity of the situation was considered.

"Sam, we're really sorry about all of this," Jenny replied softly, breaking the uncomfortable silence. "Jim and I don't know anything about bed-and-breakfasts, or what it's like to walk in your shoes without Roger beside you. But we want to be there for you if you are having problems. You know how things usually move so slowly around here. There is always a lot of talk before any action. And most of the time, there is just a lot of talk, period."

"Talk? So have you been hearing things? Are people complaining about me?"

"You remember how it is in Freedom," Jim said. "Of course we *hear* things. That's just the way it is in a small town. Everyone has an opinion, and they don't mind sharing it, either."

"What are people saying about me, about Sweetland?" Sam inquired.

"Some good things," Jenny jumped in, trying to sound upbeat. "Some folks are really happy that you are here and think it's great for the whole town."

"*Some* people, OK, I get that," Sam said. "What about the others? You are being a bit mysterious, Jen."

"Honestly, I don't think it's you, Sam. Some of the others just can't stand any sort of change," Jim told her. "People—you know how they are. And then there are those who are just plain jealous over the fact that you got the Foster place."

"Jealous? Of me? Let's see now. My husband is dead, my finances are a mess, my future is uncertain, and my son is mad. I lost a job that I loved and thought I would have until I retired. And, if all of that isn't enough, my boss told me I was a fool, and yes, she also told me that people in this little dot on the map would run me out of here. Turns out she just might be right, after all. Oh, yes, I can sure see why they'd be *jealous*," Sam said with sarcasm.

"Where do I go from here? That is the immediate question. I have guests coming in tonight, and tomorrow night, both. What do I do right now?"

The three of them talked well into the supper hour, considering the possibilities, and Sam said she would fix an easy meal for them of the United County comfort-food classics, wimpy sandwiches, made from ground beef, and a side of homemade mac and cheese, just like Caroline Jones used to make. Besides, they couldn't risk eating out in public since they needed to discuss Sweetland privately. People would be listening. It was hard to say who might hear them in a restaurant. They needed to be able to speak freely, yet privately, about what was going on and how to handle it. The last thing Sam needed was more community gossip.

Sam told her relatives all of the things she remembered about Ellen from their school days. It was a long time ago, and she liked to believe that people change. But really, it didn't seem that Ellen Madison had changed at all. Sam told them how Ellen was always so full of herself, and had that ruthless streak of entitlement.

Sam remembered how if Ellen didn't get what she wanted based on some ridiculous notion of being a descendant of the pioneer Madisons, who seemed to be legends in her own mind, anyway, then she bullied people until she got her way.

"Funny thing is, no one even knew what was so darned special about her family, but since Ellen said it was, people just believed her," Sam told them. "Back in the day, Ellen had such a convincing way about herself. Still does. Oh, she was plenty smart, made really good grades in school, was a cheerleader, on the debate team, dated the star basketball player. She was even Miss United County 4-H Fair Queen. She knew how to turn the charm on beautifully in situations where it was to her advantage. But if she didn't like a person, get out of her way. She never had the time of day for ordinary farm kids like most of us.

"I guess it was just too much for her to think of me, Miss Plain Jane Jones, coming back here and getting something she wanted so badly, even though I had no idea about that, and hadn't thought of Ellen since the last time I saw her on high-school graduation day," Sam said. "We each had entirely different story lines going on with our lives, and our paths never crossed again.

"That is, never crossed until it came to this house. Who could have ever seen this coming? Not me, that's for sure."

Not long after dinner, Sam had to excuse herself to check in the evening's guest who was just then arriving. Sam didn't know what to do besides honor the reservation.

Then, Jim, Jenny, and Sam talked late into the evening and finally came up with a temporary solution to get Sam through the weekend, at least. "To show respect for the ordinance, you won't turn on the sign's light that makes it the only lit sign on the street," Jim said. "True, it is the *only* sign on the street, but the ordinance mentioned a 'lit' sign. So if you don't light it, you will technically be in compliance with the ordinance."

They would see if that did the trick before going to the expense and great effort involved in removing it. At least it should buy them some time.

Next, she would go on and host those guests who had reservations, but she would not charge them. The trio decided to make the guests' stays complimentary and describe the perk to them as a kind of dry run to tweak things since the inn was new.

"It's kind of like how when a new restaurant opens, a night or two before it has regular hours, the owners invite in a friendly, local crowd, like a group of community leaders, in for a free sample meal to check out how everything works in real time," Jenny said. Sam would encourage the guests to share feedback with her on how they liked everything.

The guests would be thrilled that their stays were on the house, and it would get her through the weekend until she could speak to an attorney. She prayed that the Lord lead her to just the right one.

❧

THE WEEKEND GUESTS WERE so friendly and amusing that having them around reminded Sam why she wanted to be here. One couple, Jon and Cindy Knight, hailed from a small town in southeastern Ohio, and were there getting away for a weekend, much like Roger and she used to do from time to time. They were retired and enjoyed trying out the new Indiana bed-and-breakfast they had read about on a travel blog, just for fun, they explained.

The second room went to a young couple, Kyle and Ally Kincaid, who were celebrating their first wedding anniversary from another Indiana town about sixty miles away. She was an elementary-school teacher. He was an attorney. They had also seen a blog about the inn. When they found out that they would be staying for free, they couldn't believe their good fortune. Sam liked them right away.

Before the couple left on Sunday, Kyle handed Sam a handwritten note detailing every aspect they enjoyed about her establishment and thanking her for the free weekend. He said if he could ever be of service, for her to call him, and he tucked in his business card. "How sweet of you, Kyle." She hesitated. "Is today too soon?"

"What do you mean, Sam?"

"I don't want to be unprofessional by going into it right here and now during your anniversary weekend. If I did, you might have to rewrite that evaluation," Sam told him. "I've seen the detail you put into that letter, the kindness with which you treat your wife, and the caring demeanor you bring to the table. I would like to call you when you are back in the office tomorrow. I have a very pressing matter."

Jim had advised his sister to seek representation from out of town. Things here were just too close in the county, and it was hard to say who would be aligned with whom.

The best attorney in Freedom was known to be John Whetsel, but he was part of the situation via his friendship with Dan and Ellen, and he had a vested interest in seeing Sam squirm. June had said that he, too, wanted to get his hands on her house. If that wasn't enough, the legal signature on the papers about her breaking the law was from none other than Whetsel in his role as the town attorney. Besides all of that, why didn't Whetsel and Dan say anything to her about needing a variance when she bought the place?

Sam knew the answer to that was obvious: they wanted her to fail. Of course she had no way to prove it. Much of what she knew about the situation was hearsay from Mrs. Foster. Legally, no other party had made an offer on the home, so she wouldn't have any legal grounds to stand on regarding conflict of interest.

The other two lawyers in the county had been there nearly as long as the Madisons, or so it seemed. It wasn't safe to approach them, either. The attorneys, and some of the town officials, ate lunch together at the same table, at the same time, on the same weekdays at Roy Lee's Restaurant. No doubt they would have already chosen their alliances, and Sam was surely not one of them.

༄

JIM AND JENNY DIDN'T want to tell Sam this, but they had been hearing things, all right, and hoping the storm would pass. They didn't want to burden Sam with town talk. It seemed that it was not only Ellen and Whetsel who wanted Sam gone, but there were plenty of others too, from important townspeople who had nothing against her other than they thought she was too showy, doing things like placing a full-page advertisement in the local paper, getting a spread in the city paper, and even, they'd heard, getting a spot on the library board.

"Who does those things when they haven't lived here continuously for at least thirty or forty years?" one lady said to Jim and Jenny's faces. "You have to pay your dues in this town before you can be somebody. I've lived here for forty-six years, and I still am too new to be anybody."

They didn't even respond to the woman's ignorant comment.

The truth was that Jim had been taking a ribbing at his weekly card game over his "big-shot sister" who was trying to turn a dime on the town's reservoir. "Why couldn't Freedom just stay the same? It's good enough for us the way it is. Why isn't it good enough for her? What else does she plan to do?" more than one person had asked him.

He wished they had said nothing about his sister. He didn't like being put in a defensive position, and he tried to ignore their comments. But he'd about had it with them. A storm was brewing in his mind, and the next person who criticized his sister would get a piece of Jim's mind.

Still others would approach Jenny in the grocery store and tell her that Sweetland was just the thing that Freedom needed. They said that the town was a gem that few outsiders had noticed until now, when the big reservoir was bringing tourism and yes, much-needed spin-off jobs for the young people.

The folks who mostly felt that way were those who grew up here and decided to raise their families where they were raised, whatever the personal cost. They knew that they were the last generation to stay just because, more than anything, it was home.

Most people here, and in the nation as a whole, no longer felt that they had that option, or even wanted it. Their kids went to where the jobs were. Besides, they had dreams beyond where they grew up; dreams that couldn't come true in places like Freedom.

"If jobs aren't created in this town, beyond the food plant and the reservoir, and the county doesn't wake up from two centuries of slumber in both attitude and action, today's kids and grandkids will go elsewhere to live and work," one friend told Jim. "And once all the young people leave, what will happen to this place? And in short order."

To people who saw things that way, Sam represented something new, progressive even, and yet her home business honored the town's Foster heritage. The inn was beautiful and appropriate. There was no downside to Sweetland of Liberty, as they saw it.

But as in all towns, big or small, town or country, there are the talkers and there are the walkers.

Ellen was a walker. She never hesitated to attend conferences and national food-trade shows to promote the Foster brand and keep the business growing. She was plenty full of herself, some thought, sure, but maybe she had a right to feel that way. Not because of that distant, ridiculous even, pioneer link. Heck, half the town had pioneer roots. But Foster Foods of Freedom kept producing, and that meant local jobs.

What could Sam bring to the table? It remained to be seen. People were watching.

⌁

WITH THE WEEKEND OVER, Sunday night left Sam feeling, once again, bone tired. Playing what she considered a sort of favorite aunt to guests at the inn was as much a mental challenge as a physical strain. The illusion of an innkeeper was largely just that: a grand illusion. It was important, as she saw it, to appear as a combination distant, sweet aunt who welcomed her extended family to her "home" and with an easy elegance, created gourmet breakfasts that seemed to just show up each morning, and had beds that were made while no one noticed.

The only distinction between a real aunt and an innkeeper was that at the end of the stay, the guests whipped out their plastic. It was their plastic that would keep Sam afloat and let her start building an income to replace her investment and see her into the golden years.

At 2:06 a.m. Sam was awakened suddenly, again, by the noisy downspout. She had meant to call Monty about that thing, but with everything else going on, it slipped her mind. She went into the utility room to look for twine to somehow anchor it to the house. When she reached the foyer, Sam noticed the shadowy outline of a person outside the front door, looking in. The pounding hadn't come from the downspout, after all. It was from the porch.

She made her way to the front door but didn't open it. Through the beveled glass, she could make out the figure of a woman standing there. The woman saw her too and although neither of them could register details, for a long moment they stood and stared at each other's blur.

Sam wasn't about to let her in, but she couldn't seem to move a muscle to say or do anything else, either.

"I know you are in there, Samantha," Ellen said from the porch.

Sam quietly secured the chain lock on the door and opened it the few inches that the safety device allowed. She didn't look out but waited for Ellen to speak.

"I suppose you are too chicken to remove the chain and face me, and that's just fine. I don't particularly want to see you, either. In fact, I don't," Ellen said, her speech slurred.

"What are you doing here at this hour, Ellen? Couldn't this wait until *normal* business hours? Apparently you think it's perfectly fine to show up and harass people at any time that suits you."

"Samantha, you had better listen up," Ellen said in a voice just above a whisper. "In case you haven't gotten the memo, you are about to lose this house. I'm giving you one more chance to sell it to me. Unless you want to go bankrupt, you'd better call me tomorrow. If you don't, I will see to it that you are destroyed. Consider this your eviction notice."

Ellen turned, left the porch, and walked toward the street. Sam moved to the window to have a look as the woman slipped into her car and slowly drove away.

Sam considered that maybe Sweetland was actually a mistake after all. If she couldn't even determine the proper process required to operate the place legally, how could she maintain this business, all of the various guests, and make not just a living, but a new life, in this old town? She was shaking all over in the heat of summer. But this time, it wasn't so much fear as it was red, hot anger.

Then she thought of Kyle, of how she had prayed for help, and then he showed up. It was time that she stopped trying to manage life all by herself because it was becoming clear that she was not the one in control.

It was time for someone else to do battle.

And finally, Sam was ready to let him do the job.

SIXTEEN

Showdown

DAN WAS ON HIS way to his office Monday morning when Ellen reached him, frantically, on the cell. She was back in town.

"I thought that Samantha Jarrett was to get those papers before the weekend," she blurted out. "So how is it that the sign is still up out front, and I heard that she had a house full of guests all weekend? She is in clear violation of the law. Of two laws! Have that woman arrested!"

"Calm down, Ellen," Dan offered. "Take it easy, now. She signed for the packet on Friday. It's an ordinance violation; she's not exactly a dangerous criminal. And do you really have to yell at me? I got the stupid paper work done, all right. Against my better judgment of riling up this town, I got Whetsel to send it right out because you insisted."

"It's the law, Daniel; this town's very own zoning requirements. You are simply complying with the law," Ellen said. "It's much bigger than me."

"That's true enough, but it's also your own personal vendetta, my dear. When the computer-repair shop opened in Jerry's house, he didn't file any zoning papers for months after they'd opened, and not a soul cared. Still wouldn't care if he had never filed them," said Dan.

"Well, could it be that's why this is a one-horse town and the only horse that ever amounted to anything came from *my* family, Daniel?" Ellen asked, her voice wild with anger. "You screwed up by letting her come in and take that house away from me, from us. It could be the two of us living there right now, Daniel, *this minute*. And having plenty of money, besides, for anything else we wanted in life. We would have been set, Daniel. But just you wait. It will still work out just as I envision. You do what I tell you and we'll be fine."

"That's just it, Ellen," Dan said in a rare moment of bravery. "I don't see myself living in the Foster house if someone else owns it. No matter how elegant it is, it would still belong to the Braytons, with their tastes and their furnishings inside. Why can't we get our own place, Ellen, get married, and maybe you wouldn't have to travel so much, either?"

Ellen would hear nothing of his view.

"I want that house, Daniel. What part of that don't you understand? How dare you indicate that—oh, never mind!" And with that the phone went dead.

Dan was in love with that woman.

He knew what she was, and blamed if he knew why, but he didn't want to lose her.

He didn't give a personal hoot about the Foster house, or about Samantha Jarrett, either, but he cared about Ellen Madison, and sometimes it seemed that all she cared about was that darned house.

So if that is what she wanted, what would make her a happy woman, would make her happy with *him* even, he would do whatever it took. If that Jarrett woman would get fed up enough with all of this rigmarole, she just might leave, and if she left, she would surely sell the house to them to get it off of her own hands quickly, and make a profit besides.

He guessed maybe it could all work out for everyone involved.

Dan figured that Ellen was right, in her own twisted sort of way. It could all still happen just as she imagined, and no one would even be hurt in the process, or at least in the long run. It was good that Mrs. Jarrett knew that she was in violation of town ordinances. And Ellen was right: the woman *was* breaking the law of this town. If she wanted to live here, it was only fair that she played by the proper rules.

So that was the goal before them. And for Ellen, he would do whatever was in his power to make her happy. Derailing Samantha Jarrett would make her happy.

Dan and Ellen had an on-again, off-again romance for many years running. Any time it was off again, it was her doing. He was a few years older and had been enchanted with her since he first laid eyes on her walking down the runway as the new county 4-H queen. He just had to wonder why she wouldn't marry him. Maybe once they got the house, she would finally say yes.

ॐ

SAMANTHA WATCHED THE CLOCK nervously until it struck 9:00 a.m. Then she phoned the Engle, Engle, & Kincaid law firm. She expected to reach a receptionist, but instead, it was Kyle's voice on the first ring.

"Sam! I'm so glad you called. I can't imagine what's on your mind that is so pressing, but I'm free if you are. Can you drive over right now?"

"Yes, for sure, but I figured I would need to make an appointment for later in the week. I don't want to disturb your plans for the day, Kyle."

"That's the thing," Kyle said, clearing his throat. "See, I, well, I don't really have any plans or appointments. You could use some legal advice, and I could use a client."

About two hours later, they sat in his downtown office overlooking the courthouse a few counties over from United. The coast was clear; at least the coast of the new reservoir was clear. They were far enough removed from Freedom to have total privacy.

"Sam, I must say, I am quite curious about why you need me."

"And I have to say, Kyle, I need to confess something to you up front. This weekend, when you were at Sweetland, and so delighted with the free stay, well, it wasn't supposed to be like that. It wasn't 'no charge' out of the goodness of my heart.

"I bought the Foster house, and then the move came so fast, and then fixing up the inn, and in the process of all that, I neglected to get a zoning variance. I didn't even realize that there *was* such a thing. I was served with papers on Friday just before you showed up for the weekend. The papers said that I couldn't operate as a business any longer because my house is in a solely residential district. That's why your stay was free."

The attorney didn't say anything, but nodded slightly and took notes feverishly on his legal pad.

"So you see, right now I have a big old house that I've spent a fortune on and no way to make a dime from it. I'm up a creek, Kyle." Then she told him about Ellen and her threats. "Can you help me?"

Kyle didn't hesitate.

"It would seem the thing to do is to approach the zoning board and request a variance hearing. It's true, you shouldn't operate the inn until that is resolved, but with any luck, they will approve the variance, and you'll be good to go."

They got on the computer and found that the zoning board had a regular meeting that same night. Kyle wasted no time in phoning the board's legal counsel, and he asked that they be placed on the agenda to make the formal request in person to schedule a hearing.

❧

THE CALL TOOK JOHN Whetsel by surprise since he had never heard of this Kyle Kincaid fellow. Mostly folks in town used *town* people for all of their lawyering, and in the process, issues were often thrashed out among local attorneys during lunchtime over at Roy Lee's around the big table in the corner where the professionals in town tended to gather.

Of course it was done *unofficially*, but the lawyers and other town bigwigs talked plenty—long before any public meeting. They were always careful not to have any kind of board majority there so everything was on the official up and up, but still, they all knew what was going on with town business. This legal shenanigans of getting an unknown out-of-town attorney threw a wrench into the way things were properly done, Whetsel thought. Of course he didn't say any of that to the young attorney.

"Why, certainly, Mr. Kincaid. We can do that and get you on the agenda just fine. We will look forward to seeing you tonight. Have a good day, now," Whetsel said, feigning enthusiasm that he certainly didn't feel.

Then he placed a call to Ellen, and his tone was dark.

"The Jarrett woman has herself a fancy lawyer already, and they are coming to the meeting tonight."

"I'll be there too," Ellen snarled. "She's not getting away with anything. Not in this town."

"I figured as much," Whetsel said.

⚬〜๑

DURING THE AFTERNOON, KYLE met Sam back at Sweetland, and together they went to the library and looked up the ordinances for themselves and had Amy make copies, just as she had done for Ellen.

The sign seemed a clear-cut matter. Without a variance, no lit business sign could be permanently affixed to residential property. The sticky part, which was to Sam's advantage, was the wording of "lit sign." Since they had stopped lighting it, it seemed that they were in compliance. Sam credited Jim with that insight.

Now, the house was considerably trickier. Kyle explained it.

"The town law dates back decades and states that without a variance approved by the zoning board, no residential property shall operate as a business in said residential district. The exception to that is if said residential property was an existing business at the time of the original ordinance signing or if said property had *ever* served as a business site of operation. In those cases, it could either continue as such or return to hosting a business for profit, as the case may be."

Kyle said that the latter seemed a rather obscure clause, "probably added to protect someone in particular at the time it was enacted, if I know small-town motives."

It was clear to both of them that a variance was needed. Sweetland had been a private home for generations of Fosters; that much was certain.

Kyle told Sam that during the meeting that night they should be prepared to read a brief statement regarding her intentions for the property and her desire to secure a hearing date and that she should stand and read it.

After that, Kyle would submit a formal request for the hearing. If the board tried to put them off about scheduling a date, he would come back at them and press for one, and one set for as soon as possible, mentioning that the situation was creating a financial hardship on his client as she had ceased and desisted from the business operation as per the board's request.

With any luck, a hearing date would be set quickly. Before that, the variance request, along with the meeting date and time would be advertised in the weekly paper as a public legal notice. "The purpose of that is so that the public is formally notified of the request and invited to attend the meeting," Kyle said. "There, any concerned citizens can publicly state their views before a decision is made."

He explained that even though townspeople are welcome to attend and state their cases, pro or con, most generally, no one ever cared either way about such things. A typical variance passed uneventfully.

"At least that was a fairly normal model of how such things went," Kyle said, chuckling. "It was a *model* because such a hearing almost never happened in small towns like Freedom."

Sam was intimidated about the night ahead. Kyle assured her that their segment of the agenda would be over within five minutes, and then it would be a matter of weeks before anything more would happen. At least that was his experience.

"Well, if not my experience, exactly, my *understanding*, anyway, from those who have had actual experience," Kyle said.

The two sat down and drafted a simple statement. They wrote it out so that Sam could read it. She didn't want to wing it. She was sure she would trip over her own tongue.

⁓

THAT EVENING, THE TWO walked to the courthouse, and once inside took their seats.

Dan Frame, who in addition to owning his real estate firm was also president of the Freedom Zoning Board, asked if there were any agenda items from the floor. Whetsel said that he had placed on the agenda a request from a Mr. Kincaid and a Mrs. Jarrett and wondered if they were present.

Since they were the only two people in the audience, and on the front row at that, there seemed little need for such formality.

"We are present, yes, sir," Kyle said.

"Then you and your client may address the board," Dan said.

"I defer to my client, Mrs. Samantha Jarrett. Mrs. Jarrett?"

With that, Sam stood up, as Kyle had instructed her earlier in the day, and read her piece.

"Freedom Zoning Board members and attorney Whetsel, I am Samantha Jones Jarrett, and I was born and raised in this community. Even though I married, moved away, and reared a family elsewhere, I could never stop thinking about this town and its people. It became a plan of mine and my husband's to return here in our retirement and open a bed-and-breakfast. My husband died—"

With that, Sam had to stop for a moment to regain her composure. She hadn't expected the sweep of emotion that rushed over her like a strong, cold wind. But the moment, somehow, quickly stabilized itself within her, and she found herself unexpectedly relaxed. A little, anyway.

"My husband, Roger, passed away. But then I was fortunate to purchase my dream house from Mrs. June Foster, and then, everything got extremely busy, like a tidal wave of movement and refurbishing and settling in and advertising and, well, I simply overlooked the need for a zoning variance. No one mentioned it. Not one person!" she said. "So I would like to formally request a variance hearing for my property so that I may be granted it, hopefully, and operate my business, Sweetland of Liberty Bed & Breakfast, and make a living. Thank you for your time."

There was a moment of silence.

Then Dan said, "Mrs. Jarrett, it is this board's directive to you, acting as the Freedom Zoning Board, that you cease and desist operation of your home as a business until such a hearing can be arranged."

"Yes, sir. I have done that," Sam said.

"No you have not!" shouted a voice from the back of the room. Someone had entered the room while Sam was speaking because before that, she and Kyle were the only ones there other than the board members, attorney, and a clerk.

"You know quite well that you had a house full of people this very weekend right in the face of what this board, by law of this town, demands."

It was Ellen, once again delivering a surprise attack of words and accusations before Sam could gather her wits.

"May I respond to that?" Kyle asked, taking the heat off of his client. "Sirs, and ladies, I can assure you that while Mrs. Jarrett indeed did have, as you say, a house full of people this weekend, she did not charge those individuals one penny. They were guests in her home. I can affirm that to you all. There is no law against having guests, is there?"

"Well, I—" Ellen started to add.

Board member Eric Smith seemed impatient with the whole procedure and interrupted her response. "I think we can take the attorney's word for that at this time until such time as it is proven otherwise. I move that we schedule the variance hearing for the same night that the town court meets, seven o'clock, Thursday, September 12."

It was seconded, and the motion carried. Whetsel said that he would get the legal notice advertised in the local paper.

Kyle and Sam thanked the officials, and Kyle motioned to Sam that they leave the board chambers, which was also the court chambers, and the town-council chambers, and the meeting room for the Boy Scouts every Tuesday, besides.

As she turned, Sam's eyes locked with Ellen's.

If looks could kill, there would be no need for a hearing.

SEVENTEEN

Legal Notice

WHEN SAM SCANNED THE news headlines the next morning at breakfast, she couldn't believe what she read. No media had been there in person to cover the meeting, but it was apparent that someone wanted to make sure that the story saw print:

Historic Freedom home, bed-and-breakfast, faces closure

FREEDOM—Samantha Jarrett, owner of Sweetland of Liberty, the town's only bed-and-breakfast establishment, appeared before the Freedom Zoning Board Monday night, requesting a variance hearing. Jarrett had to close her inn due to violating a town regulation against operating a home as a business without town approval, officials report.

A second infraction involves having a lit sign in a residential district.

At one point during the meeting, Jarrett choked back tears, explaining that she had been unaware of the need for special permissions to operate her business.

Freedom businesswoman Ellen Madison's family roots date to the town's beginning. She attended the meeting as a concerned citizen.

"It is highly unlikely that the board will change its mind on this one," Madison said. "The board consists of five members, and I have it on good authority that these statesmen do not support a flash-in-the-pan operation that disrupts a quiet neighborhood where people want to rest and relax without commerce intruding on their peace."

A public hearing to determine the fate of the business is set for 7 p.m. Thursday, Sept. 12. Jarrett could not be reached for comment.

How interesting that it was Ellen who was quoted and not anyone in authority, Sam noted as she read the article. It was not fair that Ellen was able to position herself as the official spokeswoman of Freedom. Sam checked her voice mail, and sure enough, the newspaper had tried to reach her, but she didn't catch the message in time to respond before the paper went to press. Sam's side of the story was missing. *Flash in the pan? Disrupting the peace and quiet? Really!*

The doorbell rang. It was Sam's brother, and he let himself in. "I see you've read it," Jim said as Sam looked up from the piece, shaking her head. "What's going on?"

Sam explained all of yesterday's events. "It feels like every day in this town is high drama, and like I'm in the center of a tornado. I'm trying to come home and make a living. I am not wreaking havoc in this town!"

Jim's response was methodical. "I feel bad that I didn't think about the zoning thing, either, sis. Seems it's so rare for someone to start a home business around here, or at least for me to know about it. I just don't think about things like this."

"Jim, what have you been hearing, really? Are people bothered by my coming home?"

"It's not that you are here. It's just that you said it's been a whirlwind for you. In a way it has been for the town too. People aren't used to things happening so fast with the reservoir, the new businesses and traffic, and now the inn in place of a home that has always been there with Fosters inside of it."

"Have you been taking some flack over me, Jim? I am really sorry. I don't want to involve you and Jen in this mess, and the last thing I want is to disrupt your life."

"Sam, we're family, and you have every right in the world to come here and fix breakfasts, and talk to people, and even change their sheets if that makes you happy. If that's what you want, and clearly it is, I'm all for it," he said. "In fact, we all are. I think it's great. Obviously, you want to do this. I'm behind you one hundred percent."

Then he quietly added something more that nearly took his sister's breath away.

"It's on."

"What do you mean?" Sam asked.

"I'm not going to listen quietly to any negative comments about this house, or you in it. The next person who has a remark had better be ready because he or she will get an earful," Jim stated calmly.

She was so happy to hear him say that. At least her family was behind her.

But the five men on the board—the "statesmen" as Ellen called them—those were something else.

ﻌﻮ

ALL WEEK LONG, SAM sensed whispering around her wherever she went. Two former classmates high-tailed it away from her in the grocery store without speaking. In the hardware store, she ran into Pam, who reserved the inn in July for her own October wedding. It was a relief when she approached Sam with a warm smile.

"Hey friend, I'm sorry about your troubles," Pam offered quietly in the middle of the garden-supply aisle.

"Thanks, Pam, it will all work out. Or it won't. If it doesn't, well, I can sell the place."

"But what then, Sam? Would you stay in town? You just moved back."

"Not likely. If this town, or town officials, as the case may be, rides me out on a rail over some lax paper work, well, I'm afraid that I've misjudged this place all along. I think that's what hurts more than anything. So if it comes to that, I'll just have to find another place that will have me. But put my heart and soul into a new bed-and-breakfast? Nope. I don't have it in me."

"I hate to ask this, girlfriend, but, should I find another place for the wedding?" Pam asked, sheepishly. "I mean, you know, as a precaution?"

"No way, Pam. Whatever happens to the business side of Sweetland, the house will be here, and I'll still be under its roof when October comes. Please don't worry about that, whatsoever. I was going to tell you this later, but the time is here, under the circumstances. Hosting the wedding is my gift to you as a friend. There will be no charge and no change of plans, no matter what happens with the town."

"Oh Sam, I'm so glad you are back," Pam said, a tear running down her cheek. "Thank you. Seriously, I—we—can't thank you enough."

✑

THE LEGAL NOTICE HIT the newspaper the following week, explaining the town decrees and stating that Samantha R. Jones Jarrett had requested a variance hearing to allow her operation of a new business as part of her residence, and all parties with any opinions to express were encouraged to attend the open meeting.

Fair enough; that's the way it was. Only a bit later did Sam notice that there were not one but two letters on the editorial page. The viewpoints couldn't be more different.

One was from Ellen. Go figure:

> Editor:
> In all of my continuous years of residing in this community, having been born here from descendants of our first settlers, the Madison family, I have never seen anyone as brazen as Samantha Jarrett. She only shows her face in this town after she has purchased our prime real estate. Then she shamelessly promotes it every chance

she gets from huge publicity announcements and showing off the home online to doing her bidding to serve on our boards.

If she cared so much, she should have stayed here and raised her family, not returned here when prosperity beckons to us all with our new reservoir. Shame on her! She didn't even think enough of this town to obey its laws and go through proper channels to get what she wants. I say:

Come one and come all to the town meeting and JUST SAY NO to allowing her to ruin the quiet of our residential street with her noise and strangers.

Sincerely,

Ellen Madison, lifelong Freedom resident

The other letter was from, surprisingly, Sam's childhood friend, Angie. She hadn't even told Sam of her plans to take such a public stand.

Editor:

I have known Samantha Jarrett for most of my life. I have never known her to misrepresent herself in any way. I remember the day she moved to Ohio. I stood beside her mother, and we hugged each other as Sam and Roger pulled away. But it was Sam who was crying, Sam who called me for months after the move because she missed Freedom.

In all these decades, she has never lost touch with this community, never for a moment stopped caring about it. It has been her dream, and one that she shared with her late husband, to return here. She is here now. We are the better for it. Come to that meeting and speak up, Freedom residents. Say yes to Freedom! Say yes to Sweetland of Liberty.

Sincerely,

Angela Gray, lifelong Freedom resident

What a dear friend. Angie had never been one to seek the limelight. She liked staying in the background, seeing but not being seen. She guarded her privacy, yet here she was forfeiting it for Sam's sake.

There was no money to be made at Sweetland just now. So Sam used the time to at last rest up and finally attempt to process everything that had gone on since her return. Actually, she had barely stopped to think since Roger died. So she finally just stopped. She put everything on hold. The future was so uncertain that she tried not to let the "what-ifs" guide her. Still, the waiting was hard.

ᴄᴏ

RAY GUESSED THAT HE was wrong, after all, about his mother needing his help. She rarely called, and when she did, it was to enthusiastically share with him a success story about a blogging piece written about her new place, or about a party booking for a bunch of women in the parlor.

As the older son, he felt responsible for his mother, probably more so than his brother did, and that was how it should be. He wasn't one to wear emotions on his sleeve, so he never let on to her how difficult it was to leave Green Hills after every visit since his dad died and to see her staying there by herself in the family house.

After Roger's passing, Ray and Sally started talking about what it would take to get his mom to move out to join them in St. Louis. It would be great to have her around and know that she had them there for her. She wasn't getting any younger, they discussed, and he remembered the difficulties she'd had trying to keep up with her own parents during those years before their deaths, and doing it all from so far away. There were years when she missed a lot of his activities seeing to them.

"I'm going to approach Mom about moving out here, or at least planning toward that goal," he told Sally not long before his mom's sudden return to Freedom. He could kick himself for putting it off too long.

In St. Louis, he daily drove by a new senior-housing condo complex that was still under construction for people fifty and older. It looked like it would be really nice too. When he researched it online, he found out, ironically, that there was a sister facility in Green Hills. And what a great name too Ray thought: Greener Pastures.

He had figured that maybe she could sell out, move into a Green Hills senior condo for several years until she retired from the college. Then she could transfer to a similar one at the St. Louis place. That way, the adjustment would be minimal, the transition seamless. Her nest egg should be plenty large enough, he thought. Surely she would have an ample retirement account through the college too. Money shouldn't be a problem, and he was glad to think that she would be secure.

Just like with their finances, though, his parents had never been forthcoming with their plans. And if his dad had lived, maybe the two of them would have relocated to St. Louis, anyway. Why not? He never heard talk about any big retirement dreams. They probably just wanted to spend time with their sons, and future grandkids.

Who could guess where Gus would end up? The logical thing to do was for his mom to move to St. Louis. That's just how he saw it. Instead, she had remained alone, back in her hometown. Until now.

Ray and Gus didn't talk much about their mother's future. Ray was always the one to handle things, to have the ideas. He didn't imagine that Gus had given these things any thought.

Also, Ray had never even gotten the chance to tell his mom about the offer he had that recently rocked his and Sally's world. In the midst of his mom's sudden purchase of the house, and move to Freedom, Ray had gotten a call from a college law-school buddy back in Ohio. The friend had just inherited his grandfather's law practice in Canton—not terribly far from Green Hills. The friend planned to continue a traditional family practice there. A strong client base came with the practice that would likely remain for decades to come. He was looking for another young partner, and Ray was his first choice.

It was a huge decision, but the more he and Sally thought about it, the more the idea grew on them. It would be serving families, not practicing corporate law. It would mean a smaller city, buying a house in the burbs, and settling in to someday soon raise a family. It would mean that Sally wouldn't have to work outside the home if she wanted to take time out with their future kids, or she could work part time or from home, anyway. As the kids grew, he could adjust his own hours to do things like coach their recreational sports teams, when that day came. The move would give the family lots of lifestyle options.

But what else delighted him, and he didn't say it aloud, was that he would be near home again, close enough to watch out for his mother. That is, if she stayed in Green Hills, at Greener Pastures in particular.

He didn't want to say anything to her or to Gus just yet. He and Sally would make a decision soon about the move. But before they could tell his mother what they were considering, she shocked them all by losing her job and buying a big old house in Indiana. To say that he was perturbed was an understatement. That, and plain old-fashioned disappointed.

At least now, she did seem happy, and even successful. Ray supposed that he had underestimated her. If only he had told her about the possible plans to return to Ohio, or at least to eventually bring her to St. Louis, he was sure that she would not have made this move.

ᐧᐧᐧ

SAM HADN'T WANTED HER sons to know about everything she was dealing with, but she knew that they should know about the hearing. She didn't expect them—or anyone she knew—to show up. The court date was at a most inconvenient time. Vacation season and Labor Day were behind them; school was in full swing; people were back to their fall routines.

She decided to just lay low until the hearing. Going out and imagining that people were ignoring her or whispering to each other about her situation would only fuel her anxiety.

Despite her financial problems, Sam even took one long weekend and flew out to Denver where Gus showed her the art center and introduced her to the local culture. She needed a change of scenery. Mostly though, she stayed in Freedom, at home, alone. She would finish up some small odd jobs; iron all of her tablecloths and finer fancy work, make up several batches of the homemade laundry soap, bake and freeze the Good-as-Gold Granola; yes, even polish the silver, and wash the windows. She would keep busy, and be productive.

She reasoned that if Sweetland remained an inn, everything would be ready to go. If it wasn't to be, well, it would be that much closer to being market-ready. Either way: there would be a beautiful fall wedding come October.

But when customers called to book rooms, it was painful to turn them away. "I'm sorry," she told one after another. "I am no longer accepting reservations on those nights, but I do hope that you will phone again the next time you plan a trip to Freedom or pass through town."

It was all she knew to do. She couldn't keep giving away her services to clients. As for those who had already booked with her, she went ahead with the plans and gave them complimentary nights so as not to violate the town's ordinance. It was awkward, but she was making do.

∽⌥

FINALLY, THE CALENDAR READ September, and then Labor Day, and the week after.

"Samantha," the caller said one afternoon while Sam was on her knees in the hallway touching up the painted molding, "this is Patricia Edmond from Iowa."

"Patricia! Hello. I am looking forward to having you visit me here."

Patricia sounded troubled. "I am so happy to hear that. I researched your place on the Internet this morning, and a story popped up saying that it may close. Is this true?"

"I'm afraid that it is a possibility," Sam said. "I'll be honest with you, Patricia. I didn't realize a thing about any zoning problems until after I moved in. There are forces in this town that would like for me to lose my inn. It is coming down to a hearing. In fact, the very night you are in court over your fish issue, I will be there too about Sweetland."

"Oh my," Patricia said. "What is wrong with that little town? They are making us appear for having a short fish and you for being short on paper work. What is this world coming to?"

"Well, I'll tell you what, Patricia. I cannot answer that. But I have some good news for you."

"And what would that be? It will cost us two personal days of work and a whole lot of gas and whatever blamed fine your town issues for us to come there. I don't see the good news in all of that, but try me."

"Here's your bright side. Your stay at Sweetland is on the house. I will look forward to visiting with you, and serving you two the best that I can. It may be my last chance, and since it's what I love doing, I'm going to change your mind about this town if only in the form of the best homemade cinnamon rolls you've ever had and the sweetest-smelling sheets from my very own homemade laundry soap."

"Well, we'd be foolish to pass up your offer, Samantha. Guess we criminals have to stick together. See you next week."

EIGHTEEN

The Envelope, Please

WITH THE HEARING COMING on Thursday, Kyle thought it best to start Wednesday with a meeting at Sam's to plan their strategy. He came around lunchtime, and Sam prepared a homemade meal of her sunflower-pasta salad and cornbread muffins. A pitcher of iced tea glistened in the sunshine that passed through the dining-room's French doors. A nice breeze circulated through the screens.

"Here's how it will work," Kyle said, rolling up his white shirtsleeves and leaning into the table toward Sam. "The zoning-board president will read the ordinance and state your violations. He will ask if we have a position. I will read our request for a waiver, effective immediately. In other words, we are simply asking that your home may also be a business."

"Should we ask them to consider it right then or table it for discussion later and then notify us of the outcome?" Sam inquired.

"No way do we want them to table it," Kyle responded. "It would be easy to reject your request privately and let you know in one of their infamous letters, no face time required. I say we request a vote then and there. We state that you are losing business daily and that the board surely has heard enough to reach a decision. We push for it.

"Before the vote, they must ask if there are people who wish to address the board," said Kyle. "I doubt that anyone will come forward this time. Possibly Ellen, but she's already said plenty. There would be nothing new to add."

"Well, Kyle, it is what it is," Sam said, adding a sigh. "That is what Roger always said. It may be a cliché, but it's also very true."

"Now, Sam, I was thinking that I should put together a history about the house. You know, have some historical perspective on the property. Do you have anything?" he asked.

"I know what Mrs. Foster told me about how her late husband's family has owned this property since the early 1800s, and there is some information in the United County history book—wait! There is something I haven't even looked at yet. The day the newspaper was here, the reporter gave me an envelope filled with old clippings from the files— you know, from what they call a morgue. She said they were throwing out the old paper copies as everything is going digital, and she thought I might like them."

Sam got up and reached into the Hoosier cabinet drawer. The envelope was right on top where she had tossed it. She couldn't believe that she had forgotten about it until now.

"Great. I'll look it over back at the office and make some notes," Kyle said. "I will see you at six forty-five tomorrow night, Sam. We'll meet in the courthouse foyer and walk in together. And, Sam, try not to worry."

"Right, Kyle," she said with more than a hint of sarcasm.

That night, when Sam turned out the lights and got into bed, she felt overwhelmed by all of it once again. It had been more than two years since Roger died. People wanted her to be over the trauma and grief. They didn't understand why she still had dark moments, hours, days, and even weeks; and many people she knew had just stayed away to avoid seeing them. Suddenly, without fair warning, it was as though a dam burst and Sam gushed tears of fear, sorrow, and confusion.

Why, God, why? she asked. *Why is this happening? I am so afraid and lonely. I don't know where to go or what to do. I don't know how this will ever turn out all right. Lord, will you help me? I'm really scared.*

She had prayed about her fears before, but tonight, it was with a defining passion. Moments later, it was as though an intercom clicked on in her mind; as though the normal thoughts were on hold so that another voice could be heard; a clear, concise, firm voice that spoke to her spirit. The words were from 2 Corinthians 12:9: "My grace is all you need. My power works best in weakness."

She stopped crying.

She couldn't explain what had just happened. It seemed like a normal moment, really; yet it wasn't. And what's more, she felt this wave of peace wash over her that was beyond any kind of self-pep talk she could ever speak if she was even inclined to give such a thing. An exchange had taken place: her worry for his peace.

She noticed another odd thing.

Even though it was a windy night, the banging noise from the downspout was no longer bothering her. She had forgotten to have it repaired. But apparently now it didn't need fixing.

છ૰

THE PEACE STILL FILLED Sam's heart and mind when Thursday arrived. With everything inside her, she believed that she had been comforted, personally, by the Holy Spirit. He didn't promise that she would keep the inn, or stay in Freedom, or even that there was some wonderful *other* plan for her. But he told her that it's going to be just fine. *Surely that meant fine no matter what is ahead*, Sam thought. In fact, he had been telling her that quietly all along, but she hadn't been claiming it as truth.

But now, she was staking her future and her faith on his words. This life was not all sunshine and roses, not for her, not for anyone. But neither would she be defined by the tough moments; by what people thought about her motives, or about living in this house, or about running this business.

God was much bigger than all of it, and bigger than all of her hurts and sorrows. He would give her a future. If not here then somewhere.

છ૰

THE EDMONDS ARRIVED MIDAFTERNOON, and Sam ushered them to their room. She put them in the largest, nicest suite that Sweetland had to offer.

"It's so pretty," Patricia said. "I could just stretch out on this bed and take a scrumptious nap."

"I'm thinking about that porch and a snooze myself," Tim said.

"By all means, get some rest," Sam told them. "There are soft drinks in the fridge on this floor and a basket of snacks on the table beside it. You two have a little treat, refresh yourselves, and relax. The courthouse is only a couple of blocks up the street. We can walk together if you like. I'm supposed to be there immediately following your appearance."

"It's a deal, Sam. See you around six then?"

"Perfect."

When they reached for the snacks, the Edmonds found decorated sugar cookies in the shapes of fish. They liked this innkeeper's sense of humor.

Just as she got them settled, Sam's phone started ringing. First it was one son, then the other. She had broken down and told them everything after she finally trusted God at his word. It was only fair. She longed to be closer to them, and just maybe that closeness didn't start with them, after all. Maybe it started with her. Maybe it was about being more open about her life, and about even the parts that weren't so great. She now felt a new closeness to her boys and to Sally that she hadn't in quite a while.

"I'm doing well," Sam told her sons, and meant it.

Then Jim and Jenny stopped by a little before six. "We're here to go with you, sis," Jim told her, refusing to take no for an answer. She told them that the Edmonds would be coming downstairs anytime for their court hearing and how they could all walk downtown together.

Even though Sam had this word, this new confidence that things would work out for good, she still had no idea whether she would have a business at the end of the evening. If this zoning board voted no, it was over. There was no recourse other than to wait for a new board to be appointed and petition it once again. That wasn't an option. Besides, most of these men had been on this board for decades. Sam didn't have months to spare, let alone decades.

If she couldn't have Sweetland, she wouldn't keep this house. She didn't have the resources. And fine as this house was, it was, after all, just a *house*. It was a material object. She would sell it, replenish her retirement funds, and find a job, somewhere, to support herself until she could afford to retire for good. The point of living here was having a business, and Sam could not lose sight of that for purely sentimental reasons.

When the Edmonds came downstairs, Sam introduced them to her brother and his wife. How good it felt to say *my brother*. She had waited so many years to have just such a casual introduction, to be in the same town as family. And it felt good to introduce the Edmonds as guests to her family. This was the kind of moment she had envisioned, only without a court date to follow.

∽

WHEN THEY STEPPED INTO the hallway of the zoning board-court-council-Boy Scout-meeting-chambers inside the courthouse, Sam couldn't believe her eyes. The area was packed with people—those she knew, and those she didn't know. There were Pam and her fiancé, some nieces and nephews, and standing together, beyond all of them, were Sam's two sons and her daughter-in-law.

The rest of the people faded into the background as far as Sam was concerned. There stood her very hearts. "You came for me!" Sam said, her voice giving out. "I just talked to you today, and you didn't say—"

"Mom, none of us would miss this," Ray said, hugging her. "If we told you we were coming, you would have protested so as not to bother us, and it would have stressed you out even more. If only you had let us know sooner what was going on, maybe we could have done more. We always want to be here when you need us."

Gus continued, "We always will be, Mom. Besides, we think your breakfasts are pretty awesome. We're spending the night, by the way."

The doors swung open to the room where town court would commence. There were two people with traffic violations, and they went first, pleaded guilty, paid their fines, and left the room. One was there for a fishing infraction. That, of course, was Tim Edmond. The clerk, Gertrude Hathaway, spotted him out of the crowd. It must be her thirty-three years of clerking this monthly court that gave her a certain radar. "I'm Tim Edmond, and I'm here—" he started. She finished his sentence: "For the short fish."

When the judge chided Tim for harboring a bass in his boat that was too small to legally leave the reservoir, Tim said he knew that it wasn't large enough to remove from the lake and that he intended to throw it back, but the game warden called him out on it before he got around to it. The court stuck to its guns and showed no mercy. The judge had seen his likes before. "We hereby fine you three hundred dollars." The gavel banged. "Court closed. Ten-minute recess and then zoning board convenes."

Sam was concerned. It was already past the time she was to meet Kyle in the foyer. He was nowhere to be found. She couldn't call him because cell phones were not permitted in the courthouse. Sam's loved ones all took seats near the front of the room. She excused herself from them and went to stand in the foyer. While she waited, Ellen passed her and sought to catch Sam's eye. Sam would not take the bait, and Ellen entered the courtroom along with various other people Sam didn't know.

Good thing they had gone over what was to be said. It looked like Sam would have to do this on her own. This didn't make sense. *Where was Kyle?*

Members of the five-man board took their seats, along with John Whetsel and the clerk following behind them. Sam made her way over to Jenny. "I think something bad has happened. Kyle is not here."

The gavel pounded and the board members were in place. The room was full. Sam was now seated, alone, at the front table before the board. She couldn't help believe that they had all already made their decisions; that this was just a formality.

"The Zoning Board of Freedom, Indiana, hereby convenes," stated Dan. "We have before us one matter tonight and that is of one Samantha Jarrett, operating as Sweetland of Liberty Bed & Breakfast. Are you Mrs. Jarrett?" he asked, looking straight at Sam.

"Dan, you know that I am. Yes, I am Mrs. Jarrett." The crowd chuckled. Sam wished she'd simply said yes.

"Well, then, Mrs. Jarrett, do you wish to have counsel represent you tonight?"

"I do, indeed, but for some reason, counsel is not here yet. So I'll simply state my purpose. We all know what it is, anyway," Sam said. She didn't know where this mouth was coming from. She wasn't trying to be disrespectful, but she was frustrated by the forced formality, and angry that Kyle wasn't there. Fear no longer dominated her thoughts. If God was for her, Dan Frame couldn't stand against her.

"The town of Freedom, Indiana, has determined, and in its wisdom, decreed, that there shall be no lighted business signs on residential property as stated by town ordinance. Further, a separate regulation states that the town has determined that no private property zoned residential shall operate a business without an approved waiver. That is, unless said property was an existing business at the time of, or at any time prior, to said ordinance.

"Mrs. Jarrett, you have been informed of these ordinances, have you not?"

"I have, yes," Sam said.

"What say you now?"

"If you mean, why am I here, I think we all know that I am requesting that my home may dually operate as a business—a small bed-and-breakfast establishment."

"Are there any persons here who wish to object to such a thing?"

"There are," said Ellen Madison. She was once again seated in the back.

"Then please come forward and state your name," Dan said.

After the formality, Ellen launched into her speech about how bold and outrageous Samantha Jarrett was to move into this town and try to get around the good people's rules and regulations and the intent behind those.

Addressing Sam directly, she said, "Do you not realize that these things have been put in place to protect the citizenry? To maintain law, order, peace, and quiet in our fair little town? Why do you think you can come here and do as you please, anyway?" she asked, getting increasingly angry. "Why don't you just go back to where you came from?"

The crowd let out a collective gasp at the sharp words but recovered quickly with silence. "Thank you, Ms. Madison," Dan said. Ellen held her head higher still and returned to her seat.

"Anyone else?" Dan asked, clearing his throat.

"Yes. I would care to speak."

To the front came a gentleman who lived on Sam's block, just a few houses away.

"I am Don Thomas. I have known Mrs. Jarrett's family, the Joneses, for a good many years. They are decent folks, near as I can tell, or at least they used to be. What I don't like is her coming in here stirring things up, trying to turn a fast dollar on our town. I don't like all of this foolishness. I would like for this town to stay just as it always has. Just like the Madisons intended it to stay. That is all. No disrespect to Mrs. Jarrett, but I say that it is the Foster house, not the Foster hotel. I say keep the business district up town and off of our back street before it turns into New York City. That's all." He turned and took his seat.

Dan followed. "All right then, we have two speakers who feel the town should not make a special allowance and that the regulations were put in place for valid reasons that pertain directly to this situation. That point seems clear. Now then, is there anyone here who disagrees with that position before the board renders a decision?"

The words were no more than out of Dan's mouth when hands from throughout the chamber shot into the air.

"Now, now, we would be here all night if I let all of you have a say. Let's see. This is certainly unprecedented," Dan said, clearly rattled. "Kevin, have we ever had more than two people attend a variance hearing?"

"Don't know, Danny, we almost never have had a variance hearing. And I've been on this here board a good many years."

Dan moved on. "I had a call today from someone who asked if she could speak. I told her then that she could because I didn't expect something like this. Is there a Dr. Joanna Reeves here?"

"I am here," said Sam's former employer, the past president of Frankfort College. "May I?" She stood, motioning toward the front. Dan nodded.

Sam sat frozen. How did Joanna know? They hadn't spoken since Sam left the job. She was not one bit happy with Sam that day. Told her she was foolish to run off to such a little town chasing some half-baked dream. Sam felt her face turn red thinking about the position they were in right now and how Joanna must feel that she was right, after all.

"Gentlemen of the zoning board, town of Freedom, counsel, citizens, and my friend Samantha: I saw an item in the news about this situation. When I read it, I was filled with anger: anger that my friend would have to endure this whole *trial*, of sorts. She has had one trial after another for two years, including the recent loss of her job due to my early retirement. But that is another matter.

"What I know is that Samantha loves this town. She was excited about moving here. She is a tireless worker, dedicated, sincere, and I will tell you this: I would be proud to have her returning if I were running this place. If you lose her, you not only lose an inn, you lose a champion for all of you. That is why I implore you to grant Samantha Jarrett the ability to operate her bed-and-breakfast. Thank you."

A good portion of the crowd applauded as the former college administrator returned to her seat. But others groaned in protest.

Dan tapped the gavel. "Thank you, Dr. Reeves. I will allow one more speaker."

Rising above the hands in the air, one person stood. He would not let this moment pass without taking the floor. Dan addressed him. "Sir, you have a comment?"

"I do." Ray walked to the front of the room and addressed the officials. "I am Samantha Jarrett's older son, Ray Jarrett. You, sirs, should probably know that my mother never asked me to be here. Nor did she ask my wife, or brother, either. She wanted to solve this problem by herself.

"My parents left Freedom long ago because it seemed like the best way to pursue their future together. But please know that this community never left their hearts. This town is as much a part of my mother as we are a part of her. She never stopped talking about the Jones farm, about the values of hard work and honesty. She never meant, as the lady accused earlier, to avoid any kind of regulation. It was an honest mistake. It's a mistake that she is here to take care of, right here, right now. I don't understand what forces are opposing her, or why, but I can tell you that you'll have no better friend or neighbor than my mother. Thank you."

A round of applause pierced through the crowd while others reacted silently with their arms folded. Samantha sat stunned.

"I believe we've heard enough tonight from the crowd," Dan said. "Mrs. Jarrett, do you have any final comments before we reach a decision?"

Samantha rose slowly and looked at the people who filled the room. She was humbled to see so many kind faces staring back at her, smiling, caring. She chose to ignore the others.

"I have a brief comment," Sam said. "And it's not at all what I had prepared. First, I want to thank each of you who came out on my behalf. You mean more to me than you know. My sons and Sally—you are my heart. Jim and Jenny—what blessings you are. Pam, Angie, Mrs. Conner—you are dear friends. Dr. Reeves—I'm speechless.

"Zoning-board members, please know that I would dearly love to keep my home and operate it as a business. But no matter how this thing turns out, I know that it will be *just fine*. Do as you see fit. You know my position. I will accept your decision."

Sam paused, turned again toward the audience, and this time, centered her gaze directly on her chief adversary. "Ellen, I have one thing to say to you." The room was silent.

"You told me to go back to where I came from," Sam said, pausing. "Well, ma'am, I did."

With that, Dan banged his gavel. "The zoning board will take a ten-minute recess and return with a decision."

NINETEEN

Where on Earth...?

AS THE MEN LEFT the table to convene privately, the crowd members murmured quietly among themselves. Sam glanced back when she heard the back courtroom door open. It was Kyle! With him was none other than June Foster! They walked up to the front and sat down next to her.

"Where on earth have you been?" Sam asked. "Mrs. Foster, hello!"

"Sam, you are not going to believe the story I have for you! There isn't time to go into it before the board returns, but know this: Don't worry one bit. It's going to be just fine." Kyle smiled and patted Sam's arm. Then he turned and whispered something to Mrs. Foster, and with that, she handed him a bag.

There it was again: *It's going to be just fine.* It was another confirmation that everything would turn out all right.

Sam believed it, but she sure had a lot of questions for Kyle, and she hoped that the fact she was shaking wasn't an indication of her level of faith. The board members re-entered the room and took their seats. The murmuring ceased.

"Everyone, the zoning board is going to have to table tonight's request and seek additional information. We will meet again at seven on the second Thursday of October," Dan said, banging his gavel.

The crowd let out a collective moan, and people started talking.

Kyle stood up. "Mr. Frame, please. May I say something?"

The audience members quieted down. Dan Frame nodded slightly for him to continue. Everyone couldn't help being curious as to why Samantha's attorney was just now arriving. And with Mrs. Foster, to boot.

"Mr. Frame, it won't be necessary for you to postpone your decision. In fact, your decision really won't be required at all," Kyle said with complete confidence.

"Mr. Kincaid, where in blue blazes have you been this evening? And what are you talking about?" Dan said with significant irritation in his voice.

"Oh, I will tell you where I have been, but first, and of more importance, is for me to tell you why I am late and how that concerns you and my client."

Dan looked at the other board members who were glancing curiously at one another. "Go on," Dan said gruffly.

"Earlier this week, Mrs. Jarrett gave me an envelope of newspaper clippings about the Foster home that were collected over a course of one hundred-plus years. The envelope was being discarded, and the reporter thought my client would like to have the information."

"And? What in tarnation does that have to do with anything?" asked Dan, visibly upset.

"Only this morning did I start reading some of those articles, and in the earlier ones, I found something very interesting, indeed. It seems that the genesis of the Foster home was a log cabin, built on site by the first Fosters in 1801 when they came to what would become the town of Freedom," Kyle said.

"Here's the thing," he continued. "Not only was it a log cabin; it was a trading post. The Delaware Indians came from north of what is now town to that cabin to trade their furs, and other goods, with the Fosters. In fact, the Indians and the Fosters had a very friendly relationship. It was from this thriving trade—*this business*—that the Fosters earned the money to start a general store, then much later a food-supply business complex, the very one that has provided jobs continuously in this town for decades. As the years went on, the cabin expanded, built out and up, and grew into the *home* we know today as the Foster house. It, of course, is one and the same as Samantha Jarrett's home and business, Sweetland of Liberty Bed & Breakfast.

"Gentlemen, a business indeed operated on the site of Samantha Jarrett's home; a historic business involving not only pioneer settlers, but Native Americans who respected those settlers, and settlers who respected them right back," Kyle said. "Now, if you will read your own ordinance, you will see that a variance is not needed after all. Any home that once operated as a business, prior to your regulation, is exempt. Your ordinance does not say that said business had to be owned by the same person who lives on the property today or that it be the same business. It is fully transferrable. Samantha Jarrett is completely within her rights to operate her inn."

The board members looked at one another, shuffled in their seats, and then murmured something to Whetsel, who was snarling something to Dan. The audience was abuzz.

"May I say something?" June Foster asked, interrupting the growing confusion. There was not a man on that board who would even consider telling her no.

"When Mr. Kyle here called me to ask about the old trading post, I knew at once what he was speaking about. If you will check your United County history book, the one from the sesquicentennial, you will see a chapter about my family's home, and right there it refers to the Indians who came about the place to trade."

Fishing in the bag she brought, June Foster pulled out a small box containing several arrowheads. Then she retrieved one spectacular artifact. It was a carved walking stick that she explained was crafted by one of the Indians who befriended her husband's family and was made from wood from a tree once owned by the Fosters. "The same wood that likely went into the Madison chicken coop," June said, glancing back at Ellen, pointing the walking stick right at her.

"It is a matter of multiple public records," June continued, "not an opinion, sirs, that the Foster place, my former home, was indeed a trading post. It is a proud thing to know, and I am only sorry that I did not make the connection from those grand early days to your fancy rules and regulations today and all of this silliness you are putting our poor Samantha through here.

"And I want to say something else," June Foster continued. "Some of you in this room, and you darned-tootin'-well know who you are, should be ashamed of yourselves. What would your mothers think, boys? What this whole mess is about is not Samantha Jarrett. It's about me! It's about you! It's about how you wanted to buy my house, and you cannot get over the fact that I chose to sell it to someone else. Well, get over it! And get over yourselves, and let's get on with the business of this town and matters that are more important than your petty rivalries."

After another few moments of the board members whispering among themselves, Dan Frame struck the gavel once again and announced, "After further review, it is our conclusion that this hearing is void. There is no need for a variance. Sweetland of Liberty Bed & Breakfast may operate as a business as per the agenda of Mrs. Samantha Jarrett. Dismissed!"

The gavel cracked again, and the board members headed quickly out the back chamber exit. Much of the crowd erupted into cheers, and Samantha's loved ones gathered around her into a pile of one big group hug. The ones who weren't happy didn't stick around. They sped out of the building as fast as they could go.

As the room emptied, Sam turned to Kyle and to Mrs. Foster. "I can't thank either of you enough. But Kyle, we still don't understand where you were. Why were you so late?"

"How about you ask us over to your business establishment for some tea and we'll explain?" Kyle asked, unable to contain his broad smile.

"I'll meet you there," Samantha told them all.

She couldn't wait to get back to her home. To her business.

She also had someone to thank privately. The Lord had rescued her.

☙

THE EDMONDS, JIM AND Jenny, and the boys and Sally all headed back to Sweetland. Sam invited Dr. Reeves, but she declined, saying that she needed to get on the road.

"Thank you, Joanna, really," Sam said to the former president. "I hope you will forgive me for leaving you so suddenly back in the winter."

"I'll call you, Sam. We'll talk. There is more that I need to tell you," said Dr. Reeves, squeezing Sam's hands before leaving the building.

TWENTY

Tea and Cookies

BEFORE THIS VERY MOMENT, Sam hadn't given any thought to what would happen after the hearing. These weeks had all centered so profoundly on tonight's decision, on that moment when Sam would know if she would stay in Freedom. It was a clear division between one era of life and the next.

It was one of those defining moments in time: She would either be a permanent resident of her hometown, or she would be seeking another beginning, somewhere else. Either way, life would go on. She would go on. This whole experience had been trying, but she was ready to put it behind her and get on with her life; with whatever chapter comes next.

She had decided that she would not let the outcome destroy her, whatever it was. With the Lord's help, she found that she was tougher than she thought possible. But she had to admit: this verdict was just what she wanted in her heart of hearts. She would be staying in Freedom. She was elated to her core.

One thing that Sam didn't see coming was a late-night spontaneous celebration in her kitchen. But in the past few months, life had dealt her one surreal moment after another. What was one more, anyway? She was learning to roll with whatever happened. Like she told Sally, "Why not a party in my kitchen on a Thursday night?"

By the time Sam got back to Sweetland from the courthouse, Sally had the tea kettles on and, the teapots out and scalded, and the Edmonds had brought down the canister full of fish-shaped sugar cookies. Sally spread them out on a platter, and everyone enjoyed a snack.

They all wanted to know the answer to the question of the hour: What had happened to Kyle? Why was he so late to the hearing?

"So Kyle," Ray said, once they were all gathered. "We are dying to know where you were. Let's hear it." All eyes were glued to the young attorney.

"Guys, it's a crazy story," Kyle began. "When I went through the newspaper's envelope this morning and found out about the Foster-and-Indian trading post connection and that the post was inside this house, I knew we had them. It was over! And it was so wonderfully simple! This house was once a business establishment. That meant Sam could operate as a business too according to the town ordinance.

"So I called Mrs. Foster and told her what I found," Kyle continued. "I asked her what she knew about the old post. She confirmed it, all right, and told me about the antique walking stick that remained from those days. She said I could find out everything I needed in the United County Library local-history room as she was certain they had original documents.

"I thought that getting back-up support for the old clippings wouldn't hurt, so I drove straight to the library. After all, the last thing we wanted was for yet another hearing to be scheduled due to lack of information. I planned to be armed with all of the info they needed, and then some, to give them no option but to throw the thing out."

Kyle paused for a sip of tea.

"Go on," they all chimed in.

"It still doesn't explain why you were so late," Sally said.

"Stay with me a minute, guys," Kyle said. "On the way to the library, I called Mrs. Foster and asked her if she would be willing to bring the walking stick as a visual aid and her testimony to the hearing. She said she would be glad to do so and agreed to be ready at six thirty. We would head on over to the courthouse and meet Sam as I had planned."

"Yes, Kyle. I was waiting on you!" Sam confirmed. "Are you ever going to tell us? *Where* were you?"

"I'm getting to that, everyone," Kyle said. "So. I got to the library and told Amy I needed to look at the special collection of local historical papers and that it might take a while. She unlocked the special-collections room tucked away downstairs and gave me free reign. It took a couple of hours, but I found all of the historical evidence I needed—dates, even ledgers, and sketches. It was fascinating. In fact, it was all so darned entertaining that I settled in a corner out of sight of the door and got caught up in reading the documents and preparing for the evening.

"Meanwhile, apparently Amy forgot about me being down there and never did check on me, or at least I didn't notice her," Kyle continued. "Well, your library closes early on Thursdays—I now know—so someone, an assistant or custodian, I guess, saw that the door to the room was unlocked, and she locked it before turning out the master light switch upstairs and shutting down the place for the evening. The employee hadn't seen me in the corner.

"I was so focused on my work that I didn't even realize the door had been locked until the lights went out in the building, and I noticed it was after six, and I was stuck. Then I found that the cell phone didn't work in the basement room, so I had no idea how to get out of there."

Sam asked why Kyle hadn't contacted her earlier with the good news that the Foster home was an actual Indian trading post—a business.

"I wanted to be sure I had all of my facts straight and then surprise you," he said.

"Oh, you surprised me all right, Kyle—by not showing," Sam said. "You nearly gave me a heart attack. But how did you get out?"

"Leave it to your Mrs. Foster," Kyle said, bowing slightly in her direction, and asking her to finish the story.

"Well, when six thirty rolled around, and Kyle wasn't here," the town matriarch started, "I knew something was wrong. He'd said he was going to the library before he picked me up, and I knew the library closed at six. So I called Amy at home and told her there was something fishy going on."

With that, everyone smiled and looked at the Edmonds.

"Amy hadn't seen Kyle for a good long time since he was in the history room," Mrs. Foster said. "I guess something about that clicked, and she went back to the library and saw a lone car with an out-of-county license plate in the parking lot. She went in, unlocked the room, and there he was!"

"By then, the hearing was well under way, and you were having to wing it, Sam," Kyle said, jumping in. "I knew we had what we needed, so I called Mrs. Foster and told her to get ready, that I'd be swinging by to pick her up and explain it all then. I knew that having Mrs. Foster there would be the best visual aid we could produce."

"And that, my friends, is the truth, the whole truth, and nothing but the truth," Mrs. Foster said, lifting her teacup in a toast as everyone laughed.

TWENTY-ONE

October Wedding

EARLY IN OCTOBER, SAM and Jenny baked dozens of large, leaf-shaped sugar cookies and decorated them in autumn colors. Some of the sweets went upstairs into the cookie jar for guests to enjoy, but others were for something really special. It would be a first, but hopefully not a last, for Sweetland of Liberty: the cookies were bound for a wedding.

The special treats would be served as part of Saturday's catered wedding reception. Pam and her high-school sweetheart were getting married at the inn, just as the bride-to-be had envisioned it during the July open house.

July seemed like so long ago. So much had happened since.

The day after the final public hearing, when Sam learned that she could operate Sweetland after all, Ellen Madison left town, supposedly on one of her famed business trips. Or at least that was the rumor around Freedom. Sam hadn't seen her since that night and was perfectly happy about that. Ellen hadn't made any more public comments about the situation.

Besides, Sam was too busy counting her blessings to give Ellen any more mental space in her thought life. She didn't hate Ellen, as some supposed, and even though Dan and Whetsel had made her life something of, well, a *challenge* for a few months, she was determined not to harbor ill will toward them, either.

Townies came up to her in the grocery store, and at the library, and told her how awful they thought Ellen, Dan, and John were to have harassed her the way they did. As people voiced their views, they eagerly watched Sam's face, searching for signs of latent distress or current victory, and certainly expecting her to agree with their assessments and start complaining about their putting her through so much pointless trauma.

But instead, Sam took them aback when she refused to bad-mouth the trio, or even complain about her own treatment. She wouldn't hand out negative sound bites to be repeated around town. Burnt bridges were hard to rebuild.

Aside from the whole ordinance mess, she could understand that even though Sweetland was then, and remained now, her dream, that didn't mean other people couldn't have their own dreams too. On some level, she understood how her arrival on the scene ruined some other people's hopes for their own futures and shook things up.

"I really should have looked into all of the ins and outs of inn-keeping, including the legalities, before I took on such a challenge," she told those who asked about the turmoil. "But I think we've finally got things smoothed out. Send your friends and family to check us out when they need a place to check in," she would cheerfully tell the naysayers, as well as those who simply wanted to bait her into participating in a little neighborhood gossip.

Her comments seemed to defuse the discussion, and people moved on. There was no reason to wallow in conflict. She wanted nothing more than to put it all behind her, every bit of it.

Part of her, oddly, was grateful that things played out as they did. If purchasing the place had been contingent on overturning an ordinance, and the waiver was declined from the start, which it surely would have been, Sam wouldn't have bought the place. She most certainly wouldn't have had Kyle Kincaid around to put together the trading-post connection. The dream of an inn would never have become a reality.

While Sam knew, vaguely, from her readings, that the Fosters once had a trading post, she never would have thought about it in terms of a *business* relating in any way to the regulation.

Looking back on the whole picture made her certain that it was all part of God's plan to work it all out for her good. She was filled with gratitude and amazed at his mysterious ways. She would forevermore give him the glory.

Aside from forgiving the hassle she had been through, Sam knew there was a pragmatic side to the situation. The four of them—Ellen, Dan, John, and Sam—would likely remain in this town, and in one another's lives, for as long as any of them lived, which could be quite a long time. She was determined to move forward and get along with them in the years to come. She refused to waste any amount of time and energy being bitter.

Sam believed that folks are commanded to forgive as they are forgiven, and that was just what she planned to do. She prayed that her rivals felt now, or would come to feel, the same.

But on the other hand, she wasn't commanded to be their best friends, either. And she was not in any hurry to see any of them. In fact, she looked forward to a period of simply minding her own business, literally, as she cared for guests, prepared breakfasts, and carried on. It was time to live her new, normal life after all the considerable drama of recent months.

After careful consideration, Sam turned down the formal request to serve on the library board, at least for now, and wasn't seeking any new publicity of any kind, thank you very much. Besides deciding that she would attend the Freedom Community Church downtown on Sundays after all, she planned to put a hold on joining any other organizations, or taking on any committee work. That all might well come later, but for now, she needed to simply settle in and be still. She needed to get comfortable with her role as innkeeper.

She wanted some porch time.

As for publicity, she had garnered enough headlines, whether about decorating, or courthouse matters, and she wasn't any longer accepting interviews with newspapers, magazines, bloggers, or radio stations. Maybe down the road she would start her own blog about the inn. It might even be fun.

The Gazette reporter had attended the variance hearing, taking it all in, and the next weekend a front-page feature story detailed the whole crazy tale about how Samantha needed to thank the Native Americans for saving her inn.

The article generated such an unexpected reaction that Sam heard from quite a few high-profile media outlets, and the bookings were still rolling in from the story. And quite an unusual story it was, she had to admit.

History-loving guests wanted to see the place, and especially view the one small room in the back of the house, a mud room of sorts, where the original structure served as the trading post.

It gave Sam an idea. Maybe she could clear out the room and make it into a small gift shop stocked with arts and crafts produced by local artisans.

The reservoir was getting publicity and Sam hoped that area businesses were somehow benefitting as a result of both points of interest. Local tourism meant that people bought food and gas while they were in town.

But enough was enough. She had plenty of reservations, and she even had to turn people away. While she was more than happy to fill the place most every night of the week, she wanted at least one night out of seven off so that she could spend the time with Jim and Jenny, and the extended Jones family, or just relax. It was time that she got to better know her relatives.

And, she wanted to explore the area and see what had changed through the years; take a boat ride on that reservoir, for heaven's sake. Samantha wanted to finally live a quiet, productive life on North Main Street in her home. *Her home.* The phrase still warmed her heart.

Already, she was planning how to decorate the house for the holidays. It would be her first Christmas at Sweetland. Christmastime had always been her favorite part of year, and this one was extra special. She envisioned wreaths with simple red ribbons in every window, a huge tree positioned in the front right parlor so that it was seen from passersby on North Main Street, and a tree in the middle of the porch gazebo too. Naturally, she would get the trees from her brother's very own Christmas-tree farm.

And good news came from her kids. Ray, Sally, and Gus would be spending Christmas with her in Freedom. They said they didn't want to miss out on her favorite major holiday, especially after all she had been through. She was so excited. They hadn't all been together for Christmas since Roger's last year with them.

But that wasn't the best of it.

Ray had told Sam not to say anything, and that it would have to wait until Christmas when they told everyone at once, but he and Sally had some special news to share.

Call it a mother's intuition, but Sam was pretty sure they were going to announce an addition to the family. It was hard to wait for the official word, but it was exciting to think about the possibility of becoming a grandmother. She could tell by her older son's voice that he was happy—happier, in fact, than he had seemed in a long time. It delighted her to know that serious-minded Ray was so joyful. So she would just have to wait. Still, crocheting some booties and baby blankets during the evening hours wouldn't hurt anyone.

She had been asked to have Sweetland featured on the literary club's annual fundraiser-holiday home tour, but declined on the spot.

"Not this year, ladies," Sam told the women. "This year has had enough open houses, special events, and publicity tours for anyone. I'm going to concentrate on my paid guests for a while—and on my crocheting. Maybe you'll ask me again in a couple of years, and I will probably agree, but not this time. I am flattered, though, gals. Thank you."

⁓

JOANNA REEVES BOOKED THE inn for one night, a week after the big hearing, and the two old colleagues sat up late talking about their decade of working together, the plans Joanna had for her new retirement, and those that Sam had for her new place.

Sam learned something that Joanna felt she couldn't share back in February, or even until now. The retirement announcement that rocked Sam's world suddenly, and amazingly, made sense when explained quietly, and thoughtfully, in the quiet of the Sweetland parlor.

"I felt that I couldn't tell you or anyone back then," Joanna confided to Sam, "but my husband, Bob, has cancer. He insisted that no one know at the time of his diagnosis back in January. Remember those personal days I took in the days before my resignation? Well, I was with him at the hospital."

"Oh, Joanna, no! I'm so sorry," Sam said.

"It's OK," said her former boss. "He's doing well now, very well, in fact. We both are. In fact, while you were busy moving in the spring, he was in the middle of treatments. It was a difficult time for us, and my reaction was to shut out everyone and everything.

"We decided in early winter that we had both put our personal lives on hold for far too many decades and that we needed to spend time together—as much time as possible—while we were still able," the former college president continued. "That is why I announced my retirement so suddenly, and also why I felt I had to be silent about the details. That day I announced it, when you came into my office and wanted to talk about it, I just couldn't. When I turned my back on you, it was wrong. But it was to hide my tears. I was terrified."

"Joanna," Sam said softly. "I didn't know; I had no idea. I am so sorry for what you and Bob were going through, for what you are both still going through."

"I know. And I know that I handled it badly. I guess being around you reminded me that I could lose my husband too like you lost Roger," Joanna said. "It's not right. It's no justification. It's just that's how I felt then, and why I was so short with you, Samantha. I just couldn't talk to you about it then. I do apologize."

It all finally made sense. At once, Sam understood the coolness, the unexpected resignation, and the way Joanna brushed her off. She also comprehended Joanna's need both for privacy, and for more time, as much time as she could possibly manage, with her husband.

If Sam had it to do over, could have seen it coming, she would have relished every moment with Roger, and not let small things upset her.

Life was indeed short, and precious. These were facts of life that it often took until late middle age to fully comprehend.

Dr. Reeves also confided that when she made the snide comment about Sweetland, and the town of Freedom, it was out of her own fear. "I saw you go through the painful aftermath of losing Roger, and then getting ready to start a whole new life. With Bob's cancer, I just didn't want to see all of that. I feared the same loss you experienced. You wanted a new life because Roger was gone. I didn't want to look at a new life while hoping, praying, to keep my old one. Can you ever forgive me, Sam?"

"Joanna, I already have! I'll never think of it again. You know, God specializes in working things out. Even though everything happened at once, and at times I questioned if I was on the right path moving back here, now I feel sure that I was. I'm just so glad that your husband is doing well these days."

⁓

PAM LOOKED RADIANT IN her simple white gown as she glided down Sweetland's open staircase that sunny October afternoon. Her beaming bridegroom met her at the main-floor landing, the same place where Sam stood when June Foster invited her into the house for the first time. It hadn't even been a year since then, yet in some ways it felt like a lifetime ago.

The Reverend Stan Bennett performed the ceremony, right there in the expansive foyer, while guests watched from the west parlor. It was a small wedding, with only about a dozen attending, and Sweetland was the perfect venue.

"It's been a wonderful day," Pam told Sam as the newlyweds prepared to leave town later that evening after the reception, which was catered by Sam and Jenny.

The bride tossed her bouquet high into the air, and who should catch it but the innkeeper herself! Everyone laughed. "Hey, Sam," Pam said. "It's never too late to begin life again."

And indeed, it wasn't.

As the couple pulled out of the driveway, everyone waved.

Someone must have hit the remote-control button back at the church. The bells were chiming.

Sweetland Recipes

Good-As-Gold Granola

6 cups old-fashioned-style whole-grain rolled oats
2 cups of your favorite nuts (Sam uses 1 cup each of walnuts and sliced almonds)
1 tablespoon ground cinnamon
1 (16 oz.) container of honey
¾ cup olive oil
1 tablespoon vanilla extract
1 cup dried cherries
1 cup dried cranberries

Toss together oats, nuts, and cinnamon. Set aside in large bowl.

In separate bowl, whisk honey, oil, and vanilla. Add wet mixture to dry mixture and blend well.

Lightly spray oil on two baking sheets. Spread the granola evenly on the sheets and bake at 350 degrees for 20 minutes. Remove from oven; loosen and stir granola. Reduce heat to 225 degrees and bake again for one hour (or so), stirring a couple of times during the hour. Granola should be crunchy and golden when ready.

Remove baking sheets from oven and allow granola to cool. When it has reached room temperature, scrape it from sheets into a bowl and add the dried fruit; mix well. Store the granola mixture in an airtight container. Serve as cereal with milk or with yogurt and fresh fruit as a parfait. Or, if you are looking for a smile, bag it up and send it home with guests. Freezes well.

Makes about 10 cups.

Samantha got the original recipe from her Green Hills friend, Gay. Gay got it from her mother, Betty Greenwood. Sam tweaked the recipe to her own taste and keeps it on hand at Sweetland all the time for a popular breakfast cereal. If she has any on hand, she adds her brother Jim's hazelnuts in place of the almonds. (He and Jenny grow them on their farm.) Guests enjoy taking bags of the granola home after their visits. Why? Because it's as good as gold.

❧

Cheryl's Mexican Dip

1 lb. hot or mild sausage, to taste (Cheryl prefers hot)
½ cup sour cream
½ cup hot or mild salsa
1 cup shredded cheddar cheese
½ cup shredded mozzarella cheese

Brown sausage and drain off the grease. Combine sour cream, salsa, and the cheddar cheese. Stir sour-cream mixture in with sausage. Pour into baking dish. Sprinkle with the mozzarella cheese. Bake 15-to-20 minutes at 350 degrees. Serve with tortilla chips.

This hot appetizer has been made "forever" by Sam's friend Cheryl. Roger and Sam's sons have always remarked favorably when they've enjoyed it, and Gus requested it for the Sweetland open house. Cheryl prepared it that day for the guests. There were no leftovers.

❧

Sam's Sunflower-Chicken Pasta Salad

1 box (16 oz.) tricolor twist pasta
¼ cup salted sunflower kernels

1 bunch fresh broccoli, cut up
1 fresh red pepper, cut up
1 fresh green pepper, cut up
1 cup shredded carrots
1 bottle (16 oz.) Ranch dressing
2 cups chunked or shredded pieces of cooked chicken breast

Cook pasta according to package directions. Rinse, drain, and place in large bowl. Add sunflower kernels, cut-up veggies, chicken, and Ranch dressing. Toss those ingredients. Cover and chill until ready to serve.

Everyone needs a go-to dish, and this is one of Sam's. The salad keeps great in the fridge, so it can be made the day before it is needed. Sam served this to Kyle when they met at Sweetland to discuss the hearing. There was plenty left for her own dinner and even for the next day's lunch.

℮〜

United County Wimpy

1 pound hamburger
¼ cup ketchup
1 tablespoon Worcestershire sauce
¼ cup brown sugar
1 small onion, chopped
1 small green pepper, chopped
Salt and pepper to taste

Brown hamburger and cook chopped vegetables with it until tender; drain off all grease. Whisk together in separate bowl the ketchup, Worcestershire sauce, brown sugar, salt, and pepper. Add wet mixture to meat mixture and heat on low until mixture is hot. Serve on buns.

Wimpy is a classic in Freedom. You'll have it in homes for meals, or at public events such as farm auctions and church suppers. Wimpy is basically a homemade sloppy joe—only better. Everyone makes it a little bit differently. This recipe was tweaked by Sam after coming to her from her sister-in-law, Jenny.

⤳

Sweetland of Liberty Signature Sugar Cookies

$^2/_3$ cup solid vegetable shortening
¾ cup sugar
½ teaspoon grated orange peel
½ teaspoon vanilla
1 large egg
4 teaspoons milk
2 cups flour
1 ½ teaspoon baking powder
¼ teaspoon salt
*4 cups of love

Thoroughly cream vegetable shortening, sugar, orange peel, and vanilla. Add egg; beat until light and fluffy at medium speed for two minutes. Stir in milk. In separate bowl sift together dry ingredients. Add half the love. Blend dry ingredients into cream mixture. Divide dough into half; chill in refrigerator for one hour (no longer).

After an hour, roll dough on lightly floured surface (about $^1/_8$ inch); cut with cutters. Bake on greased pan at 375 degrees 6-to-8 minutes. Do not over bake. Remove and allow to completely cool. Frost with icing and remaining love. Makes 2 to 2 ½ dozen.

* Love is the secret ingredient.

Samantha and Jenny get together monthly to bake up a month's worth of these sugar cookies in various seasonal shapes, such as fish for the Edmonds who visited from Iowa. Sam likes to keep the cookies on hand at the inn all the time for guests to enjoy. The recipe comes from Samantha's friend, Mary Pat, in Green Hills. Mary Pat got the recipe from her Aunt Martha. Delicious recipes are passed from one to another and enjoyed in new ways by new generations.

꩜

Mom's Spice Cake

1 cup sugar
1 cup raisins
½ cup solid vegetable shortening or lard
1 ¼ cup cold water
1 teaspoon ground cinnamon
1 teaspoon ground cloves
Mix above ingredients and boil 3 minutes. Remove from burner and cool.
In separate bowl, sift together:
2 cups flour
1 teaspoon soda
½ teaspoon baking powder

Add the dry mixture to the cooled one. Fold together. Optional: Can add nuts and/or fruit at this point if you want. Bake at 350 degrees for 40-to-45 minutes in a greased-and-floured tube pan. Once the cake has cooled, turn out on serving plate and serve. Or top with Brown-Sugar Icing.

Brown-Sugar Icing

1 ½ cup brown sugar
¼ cup butter
¼ cup milk
1 teaspoon vanilla

Mix and boil brown sugar, butter, and milk for one minute, stirring constantly. Remove from heat. Add vanilla. Set pan in pan of cold water and beat mixture until stiff enough to spread on cake.

Sue Conner brought this old-fashioned cake to Sam to welcome her to the neighborhood. The cake reminds Sam of her own mother's recipe for this thrifty dessert. It was her mom's company favorite that she always baked for special family dinners.

Sweetland Scriptural References

Samantha seeks to walk with the Lord. The following are biblical scriptural references that helped her along the way.

For the Lord is the Spirit, and wherever the Spirit of the Lord is, there is freedom.

– *2 Corinthians 3:17*

Chapter 1:

2 Corinthians 4:8–9: We are pressed on every side by troubles, but we are not crushed. We are perplexed, but not driven to despair. We are hunted down, but never abandoned by God. We get knocked down, but we are not destroyed.

Chapter 2:

Psalm 143:10: Teach me to do your will, for you are my God. May your gracious Spirit lead me forward on a firm footing.

Chapter 3:

Hebrews 10:35–36: So do not throw away this confident trust in the Lord. Remember the great reward it brings you! Patient endurance is what you need now, so that you will continue to do God's will. Then you will receive all that he has promised.

Chapter 6:

Psalm 91:15–16: When they call on me, I will answer; I will be with them in trouble. I will rescue and honor them. I will reward them with a long life and give them my salvation."

Chapter 8:

Matthew 28:20: Teach these new disciples to obey all the commands I have given you. And be sure of this: I am with you always, even to the end of the age."

Psalm 27:14: Wait patiently for the LORD. Be brave and courageous. Yes, wait patiently for the LORD.

Chapter 12:

Isaiah 65:24: I will answer them before they even call to me. While they are still talking about their needs, I will go ahead and answer their prayers!

Chapter 13:

Ecclesiastes 3:1: For everything there is a season, a time for every activity under heaven.

Chapter 15:

Philippians 1:6: And I am certain that God, who began the good work within you, will continue his work until it is finally finished on the day when Christ Jesus returns.

2 Chronicles 32:8: He may have a great army, but they are merely men. We have the LORD our God to help us and to fight our battles for us!" Hezekiah's words greatly encouraged the people.

Chapter 18:

2 Corinthians 12:9: Each time he said, "My grace is all you need. My power works best in weakness." So now I am glad to boast about my weaknesses, so that the power of Christ can work through me.

Psalm 40:1: I waited patiently for the LORD to help me, and he turned to me and heard my cry.

Chapter 19:

Jeremiah 32:27: "I am the LORD, the God of all the peoples of the world. Is anything too hard for me?

Chapter 21:

Colossians 3:13: Make allowance for each other's faults, and forgive anyone who offends you. Remember, the Lord forgave you, so you must forgive others.

Psalm 107:1–2: Give thanks to the LORD, for he is good! His faithful love endures forever. Has the LORD redeemed you? Then speak out! Tell others he has redeemed you from your enemies.

Acknowledgments

A FEW YEARS AGO, my husband said he wouldn't mind spending retirement in Liberty, Indiana. "I can't think of any place I'd *rather* live," Brian said. Liberty is where we met; it's the county seat of where I'm from. I've always wondered about, and romanticized, what it would have been like to have stayed. Liberty equals home and comfort, at least from a distance, and in my mind's eye.

When I told school chum Beth McCoy about Brian's comment, we dreamed up a retirement version of our town where she would own a bookstore, we would take quilting classes—and I would have a bed-and-breakfast. Beth and I spent one glorious weekend talking about this project (and making homemade laundry soap) at The Hermitage Bed & Breakfast in Brookville, Indiana,—a joy that wouldn't have happened without *Sweetland* simmering on the back burner.

Thanks to my husband for the genesis of this book, for his constant encouragement, and to Beth for dreaming with me in the early stages.

I am blessed with our son and daughter-in-law, Sam and Allison Cronk, and with our younger son, Ben Cronk. Thank you to my brother and sister-in-law, Tim and Jeannie Jobe, for their support.

My gratitude to friends for manuscript feedback: Dr. Sue Anderson, Barbara Clark, Terri Fredericks, Jeannie Jobe, Gay Kirkton, Sandy Moore, Carol Mulcahy, Robert Reed, Marilyn Witt, Keith and Delaine Wooden. Thank you to Debbie McCray for the encouragement.

My appreciation to Joyce Maynard for one particular piece of advice, which I took. Thanks to Tim and Patty Redmond for use of a certain story line; to Betty Greenwood and Gay Kirkton for their fabulous granola recipe. Thank you Cheryl K. Bennett, Patti Broshar-Foust, and

Jeannie Jobe for the lovely recipes. Thank you to my mother in heaven, Martha C. Jobe, for her mother's cake recipe, and for so much more.

The fictional town of Freedom was used to deter locals from speculation about the "real" Ellen Madison, John Whetsel, Dan Frame or June Foster. They exist only in my mind. I wanted the *liberty* of creating people, or changing things around. Liberty, Indiana, is my nostalgic inspiration, but that's all. Remember that this is fiction. Yet if you are from Small Town Anywhere, you'll probably see characters you think you know. At least I hope so.

If someone asked me five years ago if I would ever write a novel, I'd have said no. But once *Sweetland* came, it wouldn't leave until I told its story. In the end, I'm not owner of an inn, but writer of a novel. It's probably a lot less laundry.

I must thank artistic genius (and my favorite painter) Marilyn Witt from Straughn, Indiana, for creating the Sweetland cover. She also read the manuscript and visited Liberty. I call that above and beyond.

And last but most of all, I want to thank the Lord for his guidance and hand on my life. To God be the glory.

Please contact me at newsgirl.1958@gmail.com or by snail-mail: 8754 Carriage Lane, Pendleton, IN 46064. I am open to presenting programs and visiting your book clubs. You can friend *Sweetland of Liberty Bed & Breakfast by Donna Cronk* on Facebook.

While I wrestled with ideas of pursuing agents, publishers, or independent publishing, author Robert Reed said, "Just get the thing out there." Well, Robert, here it is.

—*Winter 2014*

About the author

DONNA CRONK GREW UP on her family's corn, soybean, and beef-cattle farm in tiny Union County, Indiana. She knew as a teenager that she wanted to be a newspaper reporter. For three decades she has considered it a privilege to tell other people's stories.

Cronk has a bachelor's degree in journalism from Indiana State University. She has served as reporter, managing editor, lifestyle-section editor, columnist and women's quarterly-magazine editor while working at two Indiana newspapers, first in Attica, then in New Castle. She has written freelance pieces for various state and national magazines.

She has won numerous awards from the Hoosier State Press Association, and the Indiana Associated Press Managing Editors Newswriting Contests.

Married to Brian, a career public-school educator who has served in various teaching and administrative positions, they are parents of two sons: Sam and Ben, and a daughter-in-law, Allison, who is married to Sam.

Cronk enjoys antiques, home crafts, decorating projects, and is enrolled in Bible Study Fellowship. She is active in her church, in a life group of friends called Midlife Moms (MLMS), and enjoys lots of family and girlfriend time, along with travel. The Cronks reside in Pendleton, Indiana.

This is the author's first novel.

Made in the USA
Charleston, SC
17 April 2014